I0720825

TWITCH

WAR BROTHERS MC

BIANCA LEE WARD

This book contains adult themes and is not suitable for persons under the age of 18.

For information regarding possible triggers, please see www. biancaleeward.com or contact info@biancaleeward.com.

Twitch

Cover Photo: Shutterstock

Cover Designer: Artscandare https://artscandarebookcoverdesign.com

ALSO BY BIANCA LEE WARD

RAGE

War Brothers MC

She was mine from the moment I saw her, even if she was ten years older.

A woman in a wedding dress, drinking alone at a bar. She was stunning, curvy, and running from a betrayal that shattered her world. We shared one night—a collision of passion and desperation that seared itself into my soul. Then she vanished.

As a member of the War Brothers MC, my life is about brotherhood, fighting in the club's underground fights, and protecting the innocent. I never expected that my job at the women's shelter would lead me back to her. When she calls, in danger from the man she almost married, I'm the one who answers.

Now she's under my roof and my protection. She's my angel, a light in the shadows of my world, and she's healing parts of me I thought were long dead. But our pasts refuse to stay buried.

An enemy is seeking revenge against me. They've made a fatal mistake—they've put her in their sights. They came for what's mine, and now they'll discover exactly why my MC brothers call me Rage.

Grab your copy of Rage now.

Sign up for Bianca Lee Ward's mailing list to be the first to hear all about book updates.

PLAYLIST

Can You Feel My Heart – Bring Me The Horizon
Don't Let Me Down – The Chainsmokers, Daya
Only To Be With You – Roachford
Common Ground – Our Last Night
Reason – Hook N Sling, NERVO
We Found Love – Rihanna, Calvin Harris
You Make Me Feel – Cobra Starship, Sabi
You Space And Time – We Three
Another Life – Motionless In White
Chokehold – Sleep Token
Obsessed – Jutes
Cat And Mouse – The Red Jumpsuit Apparatus
Some Say – Adam Ulanicki
Never Too Late – Three Days Grace
Bonnie And Clyde – Phix
Eyes Don't Lie – Isabel LaRosa
Papercuts – WesGhost
Undress – WesGhost
She Got Me Like – Kode
Paper Crown – Dark Divine, Fame On Fire, Bryan Kuznitz
Numb – Ryan Oakes
I'm Good (Blue) – Jay D Stryder, Tyler Ennis
Wherever You Will Go – The Calling
Hard To Love – Coleman Lane, Zach Smith
Burning Bridges – Josh Lambert
Three Steps Ahead – Jared Benjamin

ONE
CHRISTMAS HEAT

Milly

Ivy and I have been taken hostage. We're sitting on the bed in a cabin outside of town at Opal Bay. My heart punches my ribcage as the larger man talks.

"Here's how this is going to work," he begins, standing up straighter. "We're going to the ATM. You'll withdraw money. If it's not enough, we're heading to the bank to get more."

Ivy clasps and unclasp her hands beside me. "I already told my ex, and your leader knows this too—I don't have the money. I'm not involved anymore. Come with me to the ATM and see for yourself."

He steps toward her, and a sharp whack echoes around the cabin. I gasp as Ivy's head jerks to the side. Tears well in her eyes, but she shows no weakness.

"Well," he says, his voice dripping with spite, "your ex is lying in a hospital bed as we speak. And guess what: We aren't leaving this town until we get what we came for. We're not going back empty-handed."

"I can't make the money appear out of thin air," Ivy blurts out.

I cringe, hoping he doesn't lash out at her again.

His greedy gaze shifts to me, and my stomach drops low as his lips curl into a disturbing grin. I inch back as he steps toward me. He grabs my arm and yanks me to his side. His grasp is so tight, it's going to leave a bruise. I struggle against him, trying to break free, but where am I going to go?

"Ah, ah," he taunts, waving the gun around as if to remind us of who's in charge. He stares at Ivy. "While you think about how you're going to get me that money. I think I'll have some fun with your friend."

I feel faint. The thought of him touching me makes bile rise to my throat, but I swallow it back down. He drags me toward the closed bathroom door. I scream out, "Wait! I'll give you money! I have money!"

My eyes pop open, and I sit up in bed as I gasp for air. "It was just a dream," I whisper to myself. I wipe my hair away from my sweaty forehead.

Knock, knock, knock.

"Are you all right?" a husky voice asks. It's Twitch.

I clear my throat. "Yes, I'm fine." *Oh, God. Did I scream out loud?* "It was a bad dream. I'm okay." The nightmares have been happening every so often since the ordeal. "Sorry I woke you."

"Are you sure?" he asks through the door.

"Yes, thank you. You can go back to bed."

"Okay."

I hear his footsteps retreat.

A loan-sharking organization kidnapped Ivy and me to extort money from her ex, one of their customers. Demon and Twitch found us in time and ended up killing them. I've been staying at the clubhouse ever since. It's where I feel safe, but I can't seem to shake the dreams.

I'm disappointed in myself. I thought I was mentally strong. I'm surprised by how much it has affected me. But I should give myself a break. Trauma affects everyone; I'm not invincible.

I flinch. I hope I haven't woken anyone else up. I don't want to worry my brother Reaper or his partner Ava. What had happened to me already stressed them out enough. Everyone in the MC cares, and I've enjoyed my time here, getting closer to the women and laughing at the men's antics.

The incident has also brought Twitch and me closer. He watches me like a hawk, and it's clear he listens out for me at night because he knows about the flashbacks. I appreciate his kindness and support more than he knows. I've been independent my whole life. Apart from Reaper being there when he could, I've had no one to look out for me. Twitch's support feels good . . . a little too good.

I have access to free counseling, and I would recommend it to anyone else, but I can't confide in a stranger that I was kidnapped and the man I'm falling for murdered the men who did it. The counselor would be obligated to report it. Besides, I'm coping the best I can, and I feel better knowing Twitch is there for me.

I lie back and stare at the ceiling. Twitch . . . That man does crazy things to my insides. He's over six feet tall, with thick, wavy hair, piercings, and a sexy, laid-back attitude. The icing on the cake is that he's smart—he's the club's security and IT guru. There's something incredibly sexy about an intelligent man.

But I'm off-limits. When Reaper introduced me to the MC, he made it very clear: I am not allowed to get involved with the members. I've made friends with a few, and Reaper seems okay with that. I know he's just trying to protect me—he always has tried to—but I can't seem to shake my attraction to Twitch. Flirting with him is fun, but afterward I'm always struck with guilt for crossing the boundary Reaper put in place.

I pull the duvet up, roll onto my side, and close my eyes. Knowing Twitch is checking up on me, I drift back to sleep, comforted by someone who cares.

My eyes open to the sound of squeals. It's Christmas Day. The kids must be awake. My head thumps. *Oh, dear.* Sophie's cocktails are dangerously good. The buzz felt great last night, but now I'm not so sure. I sit up and cringe. I need a painkiller. I get up, pull a pair of jeans and a top from the wardrobe, and get dressed.

When I step into the hallway, I pause at Twitch's room. My hand hovers over the doorknob. I want to thank him for last night . . . but what if Mercedez is in there? Our relationship is strained because she doesn't like how close Twitch and I are. Her hatred for me isn't a secret, but she won't say anything because I'm Reaper's sister. And she doesn't need to. There's nothing going on between Twitch and me—just my own fantasies of his kisses and what he looks like under that motorcycle vest.

The sound of footsteps makes me jump away from his door. Sophie and Viper are walking toward me, holding hands. Sophie is runway-model beautiful. Her long blond hair swishes as if she just left the salon, and her makeup is always perfect. Viper is just as striking. They would make gorgeous babies, though they don't want any.

I shake my head with a smile. "You!" I point at her. "Those cocktails were dangerously good but potent. My head is throbbing this morning."

She gives me a shit-eating grin. "They were amazing, but yes, I have a headache too."

Another squeal comes from downstairs, making us both

flinch. Jesus, the kids' high-pitched voices are going to be a struggle this morning, even though I'm excited to see my niece Hope's happy, chubby cheeks.

"Merry Christmas," I say to them and give them each a tight hug.

"Merry Christmas," they reply in unison.

"Let's go get some pain relief and coffee," I say, glancing down the stairs. "I think we're going to need it."

As we walk down the stairs, I smile at the enormous Christmas tree covered in ornaments, tinsel, lights, and bows that stands in the main living area. Everyone wanted to make it special for the kids this year.

The clubhouse is open plan, with a pool table, dartboard, and bar in the main area and a living space off to the side where we watch TV on a big screen. The atmosphere is still very much that of a space for men, but with the ol' ladies here, there's fresh flowers in the hallway and it's so much cleaner than it used to be. It smells fresher too—not like the stale beer I remember from years ago. It's a home for all of them.

I walk over to Ava, Reaper, Elena, and Axle. "Merry Christmas," I say cheerfully.

"Merry Christmas," they reply with big smiles. I give them all brief hugs and look at Hope, who's sitting on a new rocking horse.

"I love the rocking horse. It's gorgeous."

"I'm so glad she likes it," says Elena. "Axle and I got it for her."

Christmas is so much more special with the kids around. Everyone is getting into the Christmas spirit, and I'm here for it. I kept a huge stuffed unicorn at my house for Ivy's daughter Sammy so that she wouldn't see it. I peer over to see Sammy ripping through the presents, sitting in a sea of wrapping paper. Ivy is leaning against Demon, his arm around her.

I love that they found each other. They're complete opposites, but she has softened him. I see the love he has for her, and I hope I find that one day. A quick glance reveals that Twitch isn't here yet. That damn man consumes my thoughts far too often.

I watch Sophie and Viper head to the kitchen, which reminds me . . . coffee! I follow them, grab a painkiller from the medicine cabinet, get a glass of water from the fridge, and swallow the pill.

"What coffee would you like?" Viper asks me.

"A latte this morning, thanks."

I peek out the back door. "You guys did such a great job on the kids' playground equipment." They were up late putting it together.

"That was all Demon's idea," Viper replies.

I smile. "He's really changed for the better since meeting Ivy and Sammy. It's good to see him happy." Ivy, too, of course. She's become one of my closest friends.

Viper chuckles. "It is good . . . a little weird . . . but good."

"Having the kids here at Christmas is amazing. It makes it special. I heard children aren't on the cards for you two?" I ask, curious.

Sophie snorts. "Certainly not." She smiles at Viper. "I'm happy with just the two of us. I've never been a maternal person. Playing the fun aunt is fine, but I'm content with my life and don't need children for fulfillment."

I nod, understanding. Everyone's different.

"Do you want kids?" Sophie asks, raising a brow.

I shrug. "My career is very important to me, and I've worked so hard to get where I am. Besides, to have a baby, I'd actually have to have sex with a man." I can't even remember the last time I did. It's depressing.

Sophie bursts out laughing, but my vagina doesn't find it funny.

I would need a supportive, stay-at-home dad or someone who understands my ambitions and the importance of my job. I've never met a man like that. Most are intimidated or want a traditional housewife, and that is not me.

Viper hands me a mug. "Thank you," I say, inhaling the coffee's rich scent.

"So you're telling me there are no sexy doctors where you work?" Sophie asks accusingly.

I cringe. "That's a definite no. Most are married, and the ones who aren't are not my type." A lot of male surgeons have a chip on their shoulder and think they're God's gift. I love confidence in a man, but not arrogance.

"Here I was thinking it would be like all those TV shows with all the dreamy men."

I chuckle as Viper narrows his eyes at his wife. Sophie is a force to be reckoned with. She's confident and not ashamed to say when a man is attractive. She's well attuned to her sexuality, but simultaneously completely devoted to Viper.

"I'd better watch my niece enjoy her first Christmas," I tell them, and go and enjoy the rest of the Christmas festivities.

AFTER LUNCH, I'M FOUR, MAYBE FIVE GLASSES OF WINE IN. I'M ON a break from work, so I'm enjoying myself. I'm seated at the table with Twitch, Rage, and Cash. Twitch is beside me, and the other two are across from us. Mercedez is in the kitchen helping clean up, for which I'm grateful. She's a sweet butt who's always hanging off Twitch.

"Aren't you guys going to see your family today?" I ask. Since it's Christmas and all.

"Yeah, I'll head off soon to see my mom and brother," Rage replies. I notice he doesn't mention his dad. Since it's only Reaper and me, I've always been interested in other family dynamics.

Twitch shakes his head. "I called my mom earlier."

"Don't you have any brothers or sisters?" I ask him, secretly interested.

"Nah, it was just me and Mom, and I went to see her yesterday."

I look at Cash. "And what about you?"

"I'm not close to my family. All my real family is right here at the clubhouse."

My heart softens. *Bless him.*

"What about you?" Twitch asks me.

"Like you guys probably already know, Reaper and I grew up in foster care."

Twitch frowns.

"It wasn't bad. It's just that it's only ever been me and him. So all my family is here too."

"Are your parents still alive?" Twitch asks.

I wince internally. "I'm not sure. Reaper and I decided that we're the only family that matters."

"I'd better get going," Rage says. "See you guys in an hour or two."

"Bye, Rage. Enjoy! Drive safe."

Rage gives me a small smile over his shoulder before striding away. Watching him, I can't help but feel a pang of worry. The MC men have become like family to me, and with Rage being the youngest, I feel protective of him. He's like the little brother I never had, even though he's more than capable of taking care of himself.

Still, there's something about him that tugs at my heart. "Why does Rage fight?" I ask Twitch and Cash, my curiosity getting the better of me. I know the club runs illegal fights and Rage is one of their best fighters. He wins almost every match, but it doesn't make sense to me. "He doesn't seem the type, that's all. He's so kind and sweet. I've never seen the other side of him."

Cash chuckles. "Yeah, I didn't think so either until I saw him fight for the first time." He cringes as if remembering. "He's relentless. Like an absolute beast in the ring. He's so talented I think he could go pro. He doesn't even have to be the biggest guy—he's quick on his feet and with his punches." He lets out a low whistle. "Let's just say he can throw a deadly punch that leaves a man on his back, unable to remember his own name."

"Is that where he gets the nickname 'Rage' from?" I ask.

Cash nods. "He's all nice, but in the ring he becomes this unleashed monster full of rage."

"Is there a reason he's like that?"

"You're asking a lot of questions," Twitch says offhandedly.

I find myself curious about everyone. I enjoy getting to know the people here and I feel I rarely get this one-on-one time with the men. I ignore Twitch and return my gaze to Cash.

"I think it's all family shit. His dad had an affair and left for a new family. It was a messed-up situation. Rage is a good guy, but . . . pain affects people differently." He clears his throat. "Would you two like another drink?"

My heart aches for Rage. I don't understand how a parent could do that to their family. The dismissive way Cash speaks of pain makes me think someone hurt him too.

I peer at my half-full glass. "No, thank you."

Everyone at the clubhouse has their own demons. It's sad that bad things happen to good people.

Cash walks away, leaving just Twitch and me.

"Did you end up getting back to sleep last night?" he murmurs.

"Yes. Thank you for caring. The dreams still come now

and then, but I'm not as anxious. Every day gets a little better."

"That's good to hear."

"Am I really that loud at night?" I ask shyly.

He shakes his head. "I heard you talking in your sleep, and that's when you seem to have your bad dreams. Last night, I heard you cry out. It wasn't loud, though, so don't stress."

"Then how did you hear it? I thought you were one of those people who could sleep through a hurricane." He's always one of the last to get up. I'm sure the only thing that rouses him is the smell of breakfast. Twitch loves his food.

"Since everything that happened, I've been worried about you. I think that alone has made me a light sleeper."

His sincerity makes me want to jump his bones. "I know I've thanked you a million times, but you saved me that day. I don't know if Ivy and I would still be alive if you and Demon hadn't found us." The thought of it sends shivers down my spine.

He stiffens. "But we did find you. They're dead. You're safe here."

I reach over and straighten his motorcycle club vest, loving the sensation of leather between my fingertips. His cologne is fresh, like a sea breeze mingling with earthy sage. His eyes darken and slowly roam over me, lingering on my breasts before returning to my face. He licks his lips, and my panties dampen. Twitch makes me feel like I'm the most attractive woman in the world. No one has made me feel like that before.

I let go and take a gulp of wine, hoping to cool my flushed face. "I'm feeling left out. I'm the only woman who hasn't got a club vest," I joke. They're for the ol' ladies, but still.

"I'm sure Reaper would get you one if you wanted."

The women wear property vests with their partners'

names, so that's a hard no. And Reaper would never approve of me wearing anything that officially affiliates me with the club. "I highly doubt that."

He's cheeky grin says he agrees.

"So . . . how are you and Mercedez going?" I bring the glass to my lips and smirk over the rim.

With a groan and a roll of his eyes, he says, "We're not together. I don't know why everyone keeps saying that."

Is he that naive? "She hasn't gotten the memo. You act like a couple. The other sweet butts don't latch onto the guys they are sleeping with like she does, and . . ." I glance away. "I've never seen you with anyone else."

He looks away, deep in thought. "I've told her, but you're right. I should keep more distance between us. She's always been around."

I believe him. He's a genuine guy, so I don't think he would hurt her deliberately, but he is hurting her, and the longer it goes on, the worse the fallout will be. I've noticed he avoids conflict, so I assume that also plays a part.

"I've only ever been hot for one woman."

My heart rate increases. I have a feeling it's me, but I play dumb. "Oh yeah," I say mischievously. "And who's that?"

He gives me a seductive grin and runs a hand through his thick, wavy hair. I sigh. *Men shouldn't be allowed to be that sexy.* I stare at his lips and wonder if he's a good kisser.

"I think you know exactly who I'm talking about." He leans closer, his warm breath on my neck making goose-bumps race up my arms. His voice drops to a low rumble that vibrates against my ear. "It's you. It's always been you."

His words sink into me. An excited quiver radiates from my belly, and the biggest smile paints my face. Hearing him say it out loud warms my chest. I reach out and rub a hand down his arm. "I feel the same about you," I say quietly, fully aware anyone could walk in. But I'm itching to touch him.

An outrageous, tipsy thought forms, and I go with it. I look around. "You know, most members are visiting their families. The clubhouse is pretty empty." I direct my gaze toward the sleeping quarters. "It's the perfect opportunity to get each other out of our systems."

His face brightens. "Fuck yeah."

I laugh.

"I'll go up now. Meet me in my bedroom in five."

I love how eager he is. My breathing quickens. "See you soon."

He gets up, and I watch his fine ass as he leaves. I gulp down the rest of my drink. The sexual tension between us has been building for so long. After a few minutes, I walk up the stairs, blowing out a deep breath to ease my nerves.

His door is cracked open. I hesitate, but I shake my head, not wanting to think about the consequences . . . This is a one-time deal. I peek left and right. No one is around. I push the door open and walk inside to see him standing there, waiting, in nothing but boxer shorts. He's all lean muscle, with faint abs and that damn V-line at his hips. I lick my dry lips.

Time freezes.

I can't breathe.

He chuckles, striding toward me. "Like what you see?"

Those forest-green eyes pin me in place. Rules are fleeting when chemistry burns so hot it sears reason to ash. I smirk. "Yes, I do."

I snake my arms around his neck as his wrap around my back. I hear the click of the lock before he grabs my ass. His eyes light up and he leans down to kiss my throat. My head falls back, my eyes closing as a soft moan escapes me. He pulls me tighter, and I gasp as his erection presses against my stomach. He sucks on my earlobe as I lift my shirt. I pull it off and toss it to the ground. He reaches around and unclasps my bra. It falls to the floor.

"You're perfect," he purrs, his eyes roaming hungrily over me.

I undo my jeans, shimmy them over my hips, and step out of them. His eyes devour me. When he scoops me up, I wrap my legs around his waist. I snicker at the sudden movement. He carries me to the bed and throws me down. I love his playfulness.

I take in his glorious, sculpted body. He pulls his boxers down, and his dick springs free—stiff, thick, and massive. My jaw falls with a thump. Then I see it.

"Is that a piercing?"

He watches me with a cocky half smile. "Sure is, pretty, lady." He has a barbell pierced through the head of his penis. He is one brave man.

"Please . . .." I beg quietly. "Come over here and kiss me."

He slowly strokes his cock while gazing at me like I'm all he's ever wanted. As he crawls up my body, he pauses and tugs at the side of my underwear. I raise my hips, and he hooks his fingers onto the side of them and slides them down my legs. He brings them to his nose and inhales, making my face heat. "These are mine now."

He tosses them aside, moves up my body, and rests his weight on me. Our lips crash together. We're both eager. My mouth opens for him. I cup his jaw, feeling the rough stubble before tangling my fingers in his hair. Our tongues glide against each other, and I feel his metal tongue ring. He tastes like sin, and I kiss him back harder, thinking I might never stop. It's as if his lips are oxygen and I need him to breathe.

His tongue explores every inch. Desire fills me, and I'm throbbing down below. He places open-mouthed kisses on my chest, and his lips tease and nibble on my breast.

"I need you inside me now," I say through harsh breaths as a wild hunger spreads from my belly to my clit.

He stops swirling his tongue around my nipple and looks

up at me with that suggestive grin. My skin is burning where his lips just were.

"Shhh," he says playfully. "I want to spend the whole day and night devouring your body."

"Oh, I want that too, but . . ." I lean down and grab his dick.

He hisses.

"I need you," I repeat. I might combust without him inside me, and we are on a time crunch here.

He leans over, opens the drawer of his bedside table, and takes out a condom. He rips open the wrapper with his teeth and slides it on. When he comes back up, I twine my legs around his waist. He stares at me with those deep, blazing eyes. "You're fucking gorgeous."

I hum in appreciation. Reaching my entrance with the tip, he grinds forward a little. I whimper. I caress the hard planes of his chest as he pushes slowly and smoothly inside of me, making me gasp out loud at his large size. It was *almost* too much.

He shudders. "Jesus, woman, you feel so good."

He rubs firm circles over my clit until my body relaxes. His mouth captures mine as our hips move together. Discomfort turns into pleasure. My eyes close as scorching heat courses through me. He pulls back slowly and thrusts in deep.

"Oh my god." I'm gasping for air. I arch my hips, and he slides over that spot again. He plunges in, and I eagerly meet him with each thrust. Pleasure ricochets throughout my body. He grinds deep, and my body heats with a light sheen of sweat. He picks up pace, his thrusts rougher, more insistent. His palm slips over my throat and my eyes widen as he applies pressure and tightens his grip, but I can still breathe. The action, surprisingly, turns me on even more.

Amazing. Better than I ever imagined. We've waited for so long, but it's been worth every second.

"More," I beg.

"I'll give you more," he says, his voice strained.

"Don't hold back—I want everything."

He mercilessly drives into me, wild and animal like, commanding my body. The pressure builds. I'm coasting fast toward an orgasm, but I can't get enough, so I lift my hips, wanting more. This is what I've always craved—passionate, hot sex. We've been teasing each other for years, but he was worth the wait.

"Yes," I moan. My thighs tremble, and I'm clenching around him. I let out a small cry, riding the waves of pleasure that consume me. Twitch's mouth finds mine again. I have no doubt that he's trying to quieten me, but I can't stop the sounds my body demands to make. He comes with a deep moan, tensing and driving deep, holding as he climaxes and slowly driving into me a final few times. He rolls over and lies next to me, pulling the comforter over us.

That was electrifying. We're panting, but our breaths start to slow. He rubs soothing motions on my arm, which is such a contrast to how hard we just fucked. Contentment washes over me, but it's fleeting. Reality hits me like a freight train.

I get out of bed. There are a few people at the clubhouse. They could have heard us. The thought makes anxiety tingle through me.

He frowns. "Stay."

I groan as I watch him sit up. The comforter slides across his skin, showing his chest and abs. He just oozes sex appeal. I search the room for my clothes. "As much as I want to, you know I can't."

I move toward my panties, but he says, "No, they're mine now."

It makes me chuckle. I pull on my jeans, then my bra and shirt, feeling his frown on me the whole time.

"Now, you know this was a one-time thing." My voice is confident and direct, but this somehow feels like only the beginning.

His head falls back, and he bloody laughs at me. "No fucking way. I haven't got to do everything I wanted to you yet."

I squirm. It sounds like a promise. I can't bring myself to say no because I want that too, so I shake my head and walk to the door. "It's not going to be weird between us now, is it?"

"No, we're sweet."

I give him a small smile, unlock and open the door, and step outside, patting my hair down. I turn to stone when I hear a gasp. Ivy and Demon are staring back at me. *Crap. Crap. Crap.* I plaster on a fake smile, but I can see all over their faces they know exactly what we were just doing. Ivy takes my hand and pulls me aside while Demon goes inside Twitch's room.

She gives me a lopsided grin. "What were you two up to, hmm?"

"Exactly what you're thinking." I'm not going to lie. Ivy's my friend. I trust her.

She giggles and leans closer. "Was it good?"

I pretend to wipe sweat from my forehead. "He was *too* good," I mumble.

"Is that a bad thing?"

I bite my bottom lip. "Yes. Because now that I know how good it is, it's going to be harder to stop it happening again."

"Are you two a couple now? How's that going to go with your brother?"

I recoil at the mention of Reaper, and the guilt seeps in. I let out a deep sigh. "No, we're not together. You can't tell anyone." My high has all but left.

She zips her lips. "Your secret's safe with me."

"I'd rather not be the cause of conflict within the club, and I'm unsure how my brother will react, but I fear it won't be good."

She gives me a tight hug.

"I'm going to go take a shower," I say, hoping to wash away the negativity of the betrayal against my brother. But the guilt just won't let up.

TWO
AT WAR

Milly

IT'S LATE MORNING, BUT I'M STILL IN BED, GAZING AT THE
ceiling as if it holds all the answers. My head, my heart, and
my vagina are at war. What's a girl to do?

My head is the loudest, constantly reminding me of my
loyalty to Reaper. He's done so much for me—more than
anyone else ever has. He's been my protector and my family.
How do I repay him? By betraying his trust and going against
his wishes. The guilt is a heavy weight on my chest, one I
can't seem to shake.

Reaper and I were inseparable growing up. From the
moment we were placed in foster care, it was us against the
world. He slept on the floor in my room for months, making
sure our foster parents were good people. He shielded me
from bullies, even punching a kid in the nose when he overheard him calling me a nerd. He sent me money while he was
deployed so I could pursue my medical degree. He's been my
rock, my constant, and now I'm risking it all for Twitch.

After the war, Reaper came back different. Hardened. He founded the War Brothers Motorcycle Club and became its president, taking on the weight of leadership and responsibility. We still get along, but we're not as close as we used to be. He's more serious now, more direct. He has a partner and a baby who rely on him, and I know he's doing his best to balance it all. But I can't help feeling like I'm letting him down.

My heart, on the other hand, has already made its decision. It's impossible not to care for Twitch. He's so lovable, with his easygoing nature and that infectious smile. He's always there when I need him, no questions asked. After the kidnapping, he checked on me constantly, making sure I was okay. No one, apart from Reaper, has ever cared about my well-being the way Twitch does. It's impossible not to fall for him.

But the closer I get to him, the more vulnerable I feel. The more damage he could do if things go wrong. There's no future for us—not with Reaper in the picture, not with the club's rules hanging over our heads. And yet I can't stop myself from imagining what it would be like if things were different. If Reaper wasn't a factor, I could see myself falling completely, hopelessly in love with Twitch. But does he feel the same? He's been with Mercedez for years, yet he's never committed to her. What does that mean for me?

And then there's my vagina and my body—my traitorous, reckless body. It doesn't care about Reaper, the club, or the consequences. It only cares about the way Twitch makes me feel. And oh, does he make me feel. That night with him was unforgettable. The way he touched me, the way he kissed me —it was like he wanted to savor every moment, like he couldn't get enough of me. I didn't care about the consequences then, and I barely care about them now. All I can think about is his muscular arms, his rock-hard body, and that piercing . . . God, that piercing. I can't believe he had the guts to get his dick pierced, but I have to admit, it's a turn-on.

Twitch is different from the other club members, and I like that about him. He doesn't care about the illegal fights or the violence. He's happy to stay back and look after the women. The only time I've ever seen him violent was when he saved me.

But then there's Mercedez. Yesterday, after Twitch and I were together, I went downstairs for Zara and Bomber's pregnancy announcement. I celebrated with everyone, had a few glasses of wine, and tried to push the guilt away. But Mercedez was all over Twitch, hanging on him like she always does. It made me uncomfortable, and I couldn't help but wonder—would he sleep with her on the same day he was with me? I went to bed early, not wanting to find out. It's stupid to care, I know. Twitch isn't mine, and he never will be. But I can't stop my emotions. I've always been someone who cares too much, who feels too deeply. I've never been able to do one-night stands because I need a connection, and with Twitch, there's a connection I can't ignore.

The guilt is suffocating. Reaper would be so disappointed if he found out. Loyalty is everything to him, and I don't know if he'd ever forgive me. My stomach sinks at the thought. Would he stop talking to me? Would he cut me out of his life completely? And what about Twitch? I don't know much about the club's rules, but I know betrayal isn't taken lightly. Would they kick him out? Hurt him? Kill him? The thought makes my blood run cold.

We're risking everything—our families, our place in the club, our safety. My face burns with shame, but when I think about Twitch, all the consequences seem to disappear. The pull to him is so strong, it's like gravity. Ivy promised she wouldn't tell anyone, and I believe her, but it still unsettles me that two people know. Secrets have a way of coming out, and I'm terrified of what will happen when this one does.

My phone rings, pulling me out of my thoughts. I glance at the screen and see a private number.

"Hello?"

"Hi, it's Mary. Are you available to come in to work today? Jess is sick, and I need an ER doctor to fill in for her."

I hesitate for a moment, then nod to myself. Work will be a good distraction. "Sure, I'll shower and come straight in."

"Thanks so much. I'll see you soon."

I hang up and sit up in bed, letting out a deep breath. It's time to stop overthinking and start doing something productive. Maybe a day at work will help me clear my head—or at least keep me from falling further into this mess I've created.

TWITCH

I'VE ROYALLY FUCKED UP. I SLEPT WITH THE MC PRESIDENT'S sister. Do I have a death wish? Maybe. Like an idiot, I let my dick guide the way, but how could I resist? The timing was perfect. Hardly anyone was around, and I've been drooling over her for years. The men all know it too—all but Reaper. They tease me about it, but they genuinely don't think I'd go through with it. They think Milly's too good for me. And would never go for a club member.

I can't help but smile. Well, I proved them wrong because she had sex with me, and it was everything I dreamed of. Those long legs and perky breasts . . . My mouth waters. I'll never forget her pale skin against my rumpled dark sheets, her brown hair sprawled around her face, her barely there panties and dreamy eyes. Naturally beautiful—she doesn't even have to try. She wears her hair in a bun and has on baggy sweatpants around the clubhouse and still looks hot. She's a wet dream incarnate, and she wanted *me*. I was disappointed we didn't have more time. I wanted to treasure every inch of her body, to memorize it all, because I didn't know if that would be the last time we'd be together.

I was playfully joking when I said we had to have sex again, but the ball is in her court. If we don't, I think I might literally die. Now I've had her I want more. I don't think there's ever been a time I didn't want her. I can see her relationship with her brother is important, so I'm still surprised she went through with it.

She felt the sexual tension too. The flirting, the touches . . . man, even the eye contact has been intense. It's been building for years. I think she thought if we had sex once, the sexual tension would disappear. I chuckle. Now that we know how good we are together, it's much worse, so that backfired.

No one sees the playful, flirty Milly that I get to see. She acts like it only around me. To everyone else, she plays the part of a friendly but serious career woman. She's much too innocent for a wild man like me. But she's cheeky as hell. I enjoy playing teasing games with her.

"Hey, handsome."

I turn to see Mercedez by the doorway.

"Do you want to watch a movie?"

"I've got business stuff to do." I tilt my head in the direction of the computer.

She takes a step inside the room. "Sorry, no sweet butts are allowed in here." Ever since one sweet butt framed an ol' lady, they aren't allowed into the computer room. It's where I work on the computer and monitor security.

She takes a step back. "Or we can go upstairs?" she says with a wink.

My dick shrivels. Ever since I've had Milly, I don't want anyone else. I don't even think Mercedez could get me hard during a blowjob.

I give her a tight smile. "This needs to be done." I have nothing to do, but while I'm spiraling, it's the only place that Mercedez isn't allowed in.

"Oh, okay," she says, sounding disappointed. "Maybe later."

I nod, and once she leaves, I swivel in my chair to face the computer. Mercedez is attractive, but I don't see how I'm going to hide that I'm just not interested anymore. I'm a jerk for letting it go on for so long, but I enjoy being wanted. I liked acting like we were in a relationship, even though we never were. I liked the hugs, the affection, and the sex, but I never loved her. I liked having someone there.

But she wants more, and I can't give her that. I've told her we aren't in a relationship, but she doesn't believe me. She thinks she can change my mind, so I've just let it go and have continued sleeping with her. Axle gives me shit about leading her on, but I've been upfront and honest with her. If she wants to delude herself, well, that's on her.

I've noticed that she has gotten clingier since Milly has been staying here. It seems she's worried about our chemistry. But I'm single, so I can do as I please. I hate drama, especially girl drama, so I've been trying to keep my distance. I school my features when Mercedez follows me around the clubhouse, trying to sit on my lap or grope me for sex. I have a suspicion that even if she notices me pulling away, she'll only try harder. It makes me torn between not being a dickhead to her and not causing club drama.

Then we have Reaper. I groan. I feel shitty for going against his order, but do I regret it? Hell no. I'd sleep with her again in a heartbeat. All reason goes out the window when Milly is around. She has me in a chokehold. Her lips fit perfectly with mine. But there's that thought in the back of my mind: *What if we get caught? What will happen to me?*

I'm sure Reaper will want to kill me. He made it clear we aren't allowed to touch her, but oh, the temptation was just too much for me. I've always been reckless and have no self-control, especially when it comes to her. I had to have a taste of the forbidden fruit, and now I'm insatiable. I crave her every second.

Demon and Ivy know about us, but Demon keeps to himself. He's not interested in drama and club politics, so I think I'm safe there. Ivy is close with Milly, so I don't think she'll say anything either. But if more people find out . . . then we have a problem.

I heard Milly leave for work this morning. She most likely won't get home until late tonight. I'd love to spend more time with her, to convince her we need another night together. Maybe we could go away to a hotel, somewhere we don't have to worry about the watchful eyes of the club. I let out a long sigh. I can kid myself all I want, but one more night will not be enough. We succumbed to our desires, oblivious to the storm it would spark.

THREE
PUSH AND PULL

Milly

After my shift at the hospital, I pull into the shed beside the club truck. I get out and look at the rows of Harley-Davidsons. A handful are missing, making me wonder where the guys are. I've gotten used to living here. I like the club's family vibe and the company of the members' partners. I enjoy coming home to people and feeling like I belong rather than returning to an empty house. I shouldn't be enjoying it as much as I am, because at some point I'll have to go home.

A motorcycle pulls in behind me. It's Ivy and Demon. She must have just finished her shift too. Once she takes her helmet off and swings her leg over the bike, she smiles at me. "How was work?"

"I don't want to jinx my next shift, but it was relatively quiet. What about you?" I ask.

"Mine was busy," she says with a yawn.

The three of us walk toward the clubhouse. My shoulders are still tense. "I could do a wine and bed."

Ivy sighs. "Bed sounds fabulous right about now."

When we walk inside, it's quiet. As I walk farther into the clubhouse, I see Cash at the bar. In the lounge, a few of the sweet butts are asleep on the couch.

"Where is everyone?"

"Managing the fights. Rage will be on later tonight," Cash replies. The club manages illegal bare-knuckle fights and the gambling that comes with them.

I'm exhausted, but I should stay up to check on Rage after his fight.

I go into the kitchen to grab something quick to eat and hear a wrapper rustling in the pantry. As I walk closer, I see Twitch, who's leaning over. What is he doing? I step over to him and tap him on the shoulder. His body stills.

I clear my throat. "And what are *you* doing, hmm?" He looks suspicious.

He leisurely pivots. In his hand is half a block of chocolate, and there's a smudge of it beside his lip, which makes me laugh. I wipe the chocolate off with my thumb. His eyes briefly close at the touch.

I clear my throat again and put my hand out with an expectant eyebrow raise. "Share time." I could do with some sugar.

He actually hesitates and gives me a sour expression, as if sharing his chocolate is a crime, but he slowly puts one row in my hand. I scoff. "More than that, you stingy ass."

He places another two rows in my hand, though you'd think I was asking for his soul judging by his displeased expression.

"Thank you," I say with a smile, knowing how hard he found it to part with his precious chocolate.

I shove a piece into my mouth, enjoying the sweet, rich flavor. "I'm surprised there's any chocolate left." Everyone here has a sweet tooth.

"I hide it. Only Elena and Ava know where it is." He purses his lips. "But they know it's *mine* and not to touch it."

I press my lips together as I try to hold in a laugh. "Why don't you keep it in your room where it's safe?"

"I have no self-control, so I keep it in here."

"Ha! You have no self-control . . . funny, that. I would never have guessed." Sarcasm drips off my tone. I get a devastating smile showing all his white teeth in return. God, he's sexy.

"Come for a drink?" he asks, tilting his head toward the bar.

"I'm going to have a piece of fruit, and then I'll be over." I finish the chocolate, grab an apple, and take a bite as I watch him swagger out of the kitchen. He looks great in his light baggy denim jeans, fitted shirt, and club vest. Attraction to a motorcycle club member was never something I anticipated. I always liked professional, career-orientated men, but there's something about Twitch that makes me drool.

I breathe deeply before I go to the bar. I sit on the stool beside Twitch. "What are you two drinking?" I ask as I see the caramel-colored liquid in Cash's and Twitch's glasses.

"Whiskey," Cash answers. "Want one?"

My eyes dart between the two of them. I hesitate. What the hell . . . Cash is here, so we are safe and won't try anything. "Sure."

The mischievous glint in Twitch's eyes makes a familiar flutter start in my chest.

Cash goes around to the other side of the bar, pulls out a tumbler, and pours a shot of Crown Village whiskey. The distillery is owned by Sophie's brother.

Demon and Ivy saunter over. Ivy peers over my shoulder. "You're having whiskey neat?" She chuckles.

"Would you two like one as well?" Cash asks, glancing between Demon and Ivy.

Ivy waves him away. "Oh, no thank you. My pillow is calling my name."

"No, thanks," Demon answers. "We're off to bed. Have a good night." Demon's lip twitches at the corners like he's trying not to smirk as he glances between me and Twitch, making my cheeks heat. They turn and head for the stairs.

Cash puts the glass in front of me. The aroma of whiskey hits me. It's pleasant but distinct, with fruity, spicy, and earthy undertones. I swirl the liquid around in the glass before taking a sip and feeling the rich burn.

"I didn't realize you were a whiskey girl," Twitch says.

"I drink most alcoholic beverages. I'm not too picky." I look at Cash. "So, are you and Trixie a thing?" Since I live here, I'm curious about what's going on with everyone and what their arrangements are. Trixie is a sweet butt. She's always been kind to me and willing to help out around the clubhouse.

Cash shakes his head. "Nice girl and all, but it's not serious."

"I've noticed the last three single men in the club have that in common," I point out smugly.

Twitch chokes on his drink and gives me the side-eye.

Cash walks around the bar and pats a coughing Twitch's back. "You all right, man? Don't die on us."

Twitch coughs again, then clears his throat. "Yeah, I'm all right."

I hide my smile behind my glass and take another sip of my drink.

"Well, I'm off to the fights," says Cash. "If I don't see you when I get back, night, you two."

Damn it! He was supposed to be the buffer. "Good night," I reply while chastising myself.

I peer at Twitch, and his eyes are soft as he stares back at me. "How was your day?" I ask. *Just keep talking*, I remind myself, *and then go to bed*.

"Good. Spent most of the day on the computer."

"So no time cuddling up with your *girlfriend*?"

Twitch scrunches his nose. "I have no girlfriend." He leans in so close I can feel his breath on my face. "Why, do you want to be it?" he asks jokingly.

I gently push him away and laugh. "You are trouble!"

He pulls at his leather vest, a gigantic smirk on his face. "Certainly am."

Knowing I need to change lanes, as it's getting a little flirty, I ask, "So you never told me, why do they call you Twitch?" Such a strange name.

The smirk is wiped off his face. "I have epilepsy."

My eyes bulge. "And how do I not know that?" I'm the club doctor after all. "How long have you had it?"

"I was in the army for two years, and one day at training I had a seizure. It was random. Sometimes my hand would jerk when I just woke up, and I'd lose a bit of muscle function, but I thought it was nothing and would just go away by itself. I went to the hospital after the seizure, and they did all types of scans and tests, and the doctor confirmed I had epilepsy."

My heart constricts as I frown. "Were you okay after the fall?"

"Yes. It was a grand mal seizure, so I don't remember too much of that day. I remember falling and talking to the hospital doctor afterward, but everything else is hazy."

I trail my hand along his arm, giving him a sad smile, offering comfort. "I'm sorry to hear that."

He focuses on my hand. "It's fine. It was a while ago now. It sucked that I didn't get to finish my training or serve my country, but it is what it is."

"How are you managing your epilepsy? Are you on

medication now?" I'm concerned. I haven't seen any notable signs he has epilepsy.

He clips his head in a nod. "I've been on medication since the incident and have had no issues. The medication has been doing its job."

"So no seizures since you've been on it?" I ask for clarification.

"That's right."

"Have you had an updated scan lately to determine if you still have epilepsy? Some people don't have it forever."

He looks away as if in thought. "No, I haven't. I might look into that."

"Earl, our neurologist at Crown Village Hospital, is amazing. I'll give you his details, and you can book an appointment with him. I'll tell him you're a close friend, see if he can get you in sooner."

He gives me a warm smile. "Thanks for that."

"Of course." I'd do anything for Twitch. I pause and decide to ask him a question I've wanted to know the answer to for a long time. "While we're on the topic of names, what's your real name?"

"Reece O'Connah."

My eyes wander around his gorgeous face to his thick head of wavy hair, those mesmerizing green eyes, and those piercings. "You look like a Reece."

He chuckles, then brings the glass to his mouth and takes a sip. The movement makes his Adam's apple bob. I don't have a clue how, but even him drinking is sexy. I have issues!

"After you were diagnosed, then what happened?"

His lips curve down. "I got medically discharged and went home to my family."

His voice is soft, and I regret asking, so I take a large drink, and it burns all the way down. I lean closer. "How did you join the War Brothers MC?" I'm invested in his life story now.

"I was lost after they medically discharged me."

My throat tightens at the lingering sadness in his tone.

"I came home and all my friends in the army I had made were still there, so I didn't feel I was a part of that friendship group anymore. I did well at school but was never interested in college or anything, so I didn't have a qualification to fall back on. I think I slipped into a depression for a while until my mom heard of a group of ex-military men that had moved to Crown Village." He smiles sadly. "I think she couldn't handle me being miserable any longer, so she suggested I go make friends. I came to the clubhouse the next day, met them, and began as a prospect."

I blink several times, trying to keep the tears at bay. He's never told me his story, and it pains me to know he was in pain after coming home.

He puts his hand over mine and rubs his thumb over my hand. "Don't cry—everything all worked out. I made a new family, and I couldn't imagine my life any different. It's just . . ."

I wait for him to answer, but he pauses and frowns. "What's wrong?"

He lowers his voice. "I owe my life to this club. They pulled me out of the darkness. They've treated me with respect and . . ." He grabs his club vest. "I wear this with honor and pride. So whatever is happening between us, just know I'm struggling too. I feel like a fraud, disrespecting my family and betraying my president. But I can't stop wanting you."

I rub the base of my neck. "I understand. I feel like I'm betraying the only real family I've ever had. Reaper protected me when we were in foster care. He wasn't just my big brother. Sometimes he felt like a parent too. He stood up to bullies for me, made sure I did my homework, and even sent money home from the war to help pay for my medical degree."

My heart clenches as guilt threatens to overwhelm me. "I wouldn't be where I am today without him," I say softly. "I owe him everything. And it hurts—God, it hurts—that I've betrayed him. I never imagined I could do something like this, but . . ." I stare into those dark-green eyes. "I couldn't stop myself."

The truth hangs in the air between us, heavy and raw. Admitting it out loud feels like ripping open a wound, but at the same time, it's a relief. It's the truth, and I can't run from it anymore.

With a shaky breath, I drain my glass, the burn of the alcohol doing little to dull the ache in my chest. I set the empty glass down on the table with a soft clink, my hands trembling slightly.

"Do you regret it?" he asks.

"No," I answer briskly. Even though the guilt is bearing down on us, I don't regret our time together. It's rare for me to truly connect with a man, and it hurts me to think I might have to give that up. I've always gravitated toward him. "What about you?" I bite my lower lip, unsure if I want the answer or not. "Do you regret it?"

His cheeky grin is back in full force. "I'd never regret being with you."

Oh my . . . his words hit me in the chest. With him, I feel seen. I'm not just Reaper's sister or the club doctor. He sees me, Milly.

I sigh. "The whole situation is hard. Because Reaper sacrificed so much for me, I've always felt that I've had to live up to his expectations. I never wanted to disappoint him, and it hurts that I am."

"Honesty, respect, loyalty, and brotherhood are important

in our club. I don't think I'm worthy of wearing the club vest now, but being with you is heaven. And if it were to happen again . . . I don't have it in me to say no."

I inch back, my eyes wide. "Again?" My heartbeat quickens, a surge of happiness and nerves. I want to be with him again, but I'm conflicted. "Does anyone else know what happened between us?"

He shakes his head and licks those lips. "Just Ivy and Demon."

"I'd like to keep it that way. It stresses me out that even those two know. We can't have anyone else finding out."

He nods. "I know."

I need to change the subject before I do something stupid like kiss him again. "What made you become the computer guru of the club?"

"I've always been good with computers. I'm also good at hacking, so my skills work out in the club's favor because they didn't have anyone suitable to fill the role."

The hidden chocolate . . . the hacking . . . Is everything a game to him? Am I just his current fixation until he gets bored? I don't truly think he's that type of person, but I can't stop the intrusive thought. "You mentioned your mom . . . is it just you and her?"

He nods. "Yep."

"So you're a mama's boy," I tease.

He chuckles. "Sure am. I love my mom."

Aww . . . that's the sweetest.

"She's always wanted what's best for me. She was a single mom who worked her ass off. And no one can beat her pancakes . . . not even Ava!" He says that last part with pride.

I snort. "Don't let Ava hear you say that. Those are fighting words."

He smiles wide. "Did you and Reaper ever reconnect with your parents?"

"No." I didn't mean for it to sound so abrupt.

He drifts off for a moment. "Would you want to? I could find them for you."

I feel lightheaded. "I . . . I don't know. I've never thought about it, probably because Reaper was always my family. And I'm certain Reaper would say a hard no." Reaper never liked talking about our parents. He resented them for being neglectful and selfish. I get it, which is why I never pursued it. But there's always that what-if. Are they better people now? Do they regret what they did? It could provide closure, or it could go very badly.

"Fair enough. That's understandable." He leans back in his chair casually. "If you ever do change your mind. Just let me know and I'll help track them down."

I nod, a little choked up.

"Why'd you want to be a doctor?"

My lips curve up into a slow smile. That's easy. "I care about people. I wanted to contribute to the world and do something important. I want to matter, save lives, and help people when they're at their worst." There was never a backup plan; it was always the job for me.

Twitch puts his hand over mine. "You matter."

In my periphery, I see Mercedez making her way over to us, so I pull my hand away. My hand feels warm where his touch lingered.

When Mercedez reaches us, she stands between us with pursed lips. She stares at Twitch. "Let's go to bed. I'm tired."

He glances at me before answering her. "I'm sleeping by myself. I didn't sleep well last night."

Is he lying to her because we had sex and he's keeping his distance from her? She doesn't like me, and she isn't with Twitch, but I guess she likes him. I feel bad that she won't get the happy ending she's wanted for so long, and that's partly because of me.

I stand despite the awkwardness. "Good night," I say, giving them a small smile before going up the stairs.

"Good night, Milly," Twitch replies, and I feel his eyes on me as I walk to my room. Our connection is stronger now. Our confessions of guilt have been aired, and we have both agreed to keep our secret.

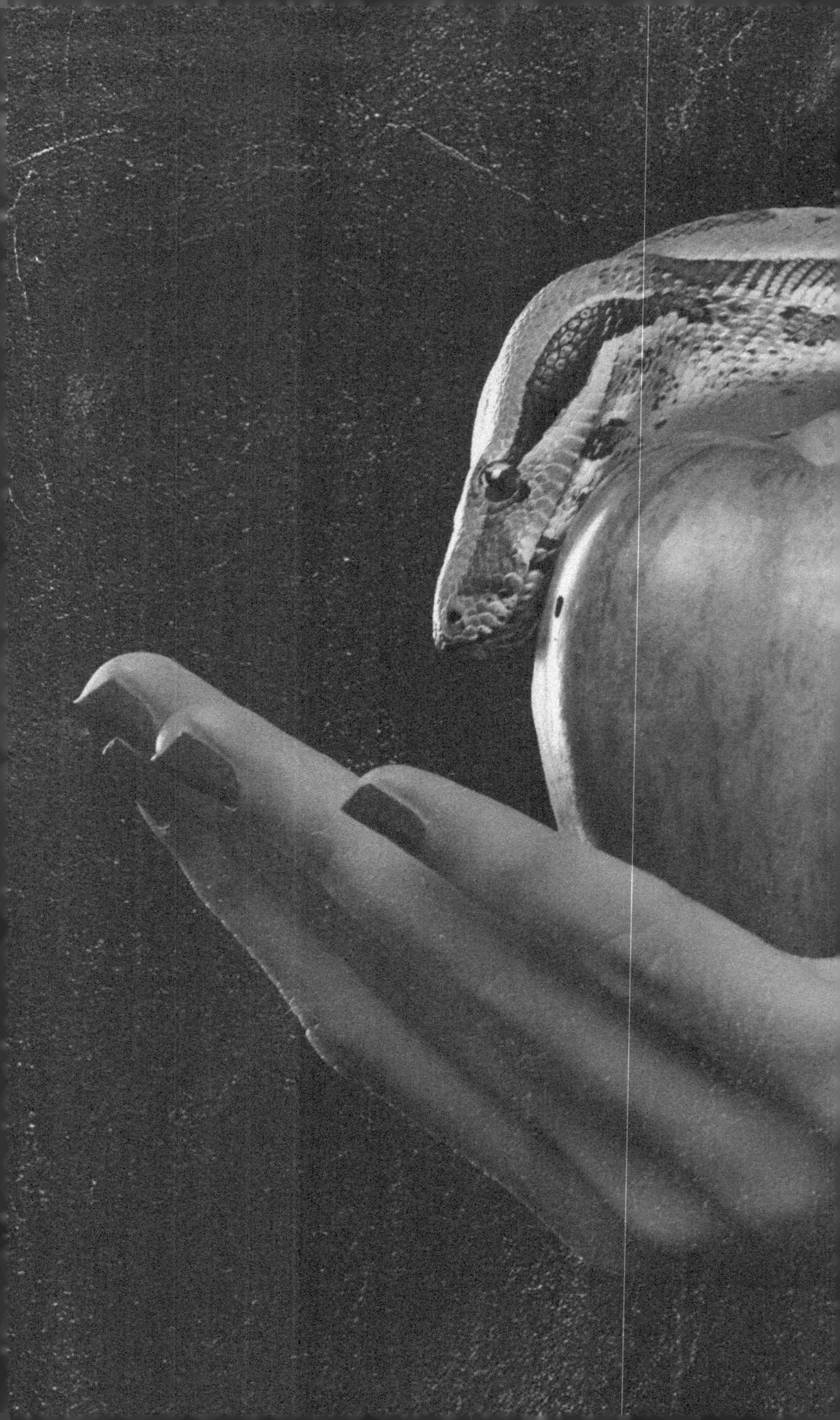

FOUR

DEADLY OBSESSION

Twitch

THE SMELL OF PANCAKES WAKES ME. I BLINK A FEW TIMES, surprised to find Mercedez asleep in my bed. She must have sneaked in. Annoyance festers; she needs to learn boundaries. I get up, leaving her there, and head downstairs. At the dining room table, I shovel pancakes onto my plate, drizzle them with honey, and pile on strawberries and cream. I take a seat and dig in. Delicious. Not as good as my mom's, though.

Axle snorts from beside me. "Calm down with your moaning. It's only pancakes."

While my mouth is full, I moan loudly again with a big grin on my face.

He playfully elbows me and chuckles. "I don't want to listen to that shit."

Milly is sitting across from me, smiling. I stretch my leg out and rub my foot against hers under the table. I should just let her be, but I enjoy our cat-and-mouse game. I brush my foot against hers again, but she doesn't make eye contact.

"Okay, who's playing footsies with me under the table?" Viper asks, and everyone bursts out laughing. *Oh, shit!*

Milly shoots me a pointed look, knowing it's me. A chuckle escapes. Being with her makes me reckless, but I need to be more careful. She weakens my self-control—she's my kryptonite.

I live in the now, so it's only when I reflect on my actions later that I feel shitty because the club is the most important thing to me and I'm putting it all at risk. I'm aware there will be consequences, but I'm torn between wanting Milly and wanting to keep the peace at the club.

I look across at her. She's wearing a fitted top that shows her curves, and I saw her walk in wearing tight jeans. She's a wet dream. I remember how silky her skin feels and how I wanted her to stay in my arms all day and night. I look at her lips and remember how good she tastes, how tight she is, and the look on her face when she comes. I shift in my seat—not the best time to get a hard-on, surrounded by the MC men, but I can't help it. I'm a freak for her, and she's my weakness.

Images of her naked body flood my mind. I smirk. If heaven exists, that's it. I can't believe that out of all the women, I'm obsessed with the president's sister—the one person who could sign my death warrant. Something's wrong with me. No one's ever made me want to be monogamous, but after having Milly, I can't even think about anyone else. Being with her is effortless. The world stops when I'm with her.

The sweet butts get up and start clearing everyone's plates.

"So whose foot was it, eh?" Viper asks, with a raised brow and a grin.

"It was me," Axle says, winking at Viper.

"I always knew you wanted me," Viper shoots back, blowing a kiss in Axle's direction.

"You're not a man till you've had a man," Axle says seductively, and we all laugh at the two idiots.

I listen to the general club chatter until Mercedez comes out and stands next to me. She holds out her hand like she has something to give me. I put my hand out, and she drops an earring into my palm. My heart races. I slam my hand closed. It's Milly's. I glance around the table. None of the guys saw it. Mercedez's face is pinched. I don't want her to say anything in front of anyone, so I stand up.

"Can I talk to you for a moment?" I whisper-yell.

She gives me a stiff nod. I lead her through the house and up the stairs to my room for privacy. After she walks in, I close the door.

My eyes narrow into slits. "What are you doing?"

She crosses her arms. "No, what are *you* doing with Milly?" She gives me a death stare.

This is the drama I dread. "What do you mean?" I act dumb.

"So her earring just happens to fall off in your bed?"

Oh shit! Panic strikes in my chest. "What were you doing in my room, anyway? I told you I wanted to sleep by myself."

She frowns. "But I wanted to sleep with you."

"You're not listening to me. I don't want to be a dickhead to you, but if I tell you I want to sleep by myself, I mean it. You don't get to come in whenever it suits you."

"I could any other time before Milly came to the clubhouse."

She's figured it out. "It's got nothing to do with anyone else—it has to do with you not listening to me," I say.

She studies my face. "Are you sleeping with her?"

"No!" I answer defensively.

"Sure sounds like it." She laughs coldly. "You'd get killed, all for her?" Her voice softens at the end.

I'd like to think Reaper won't kill me, but it's not

completely off the table, I guess. "We're not sleeping together," I reiterate.

She rushes me and pushes at my chest, making me take a step back. "You're a liar!" she barks.

"And you need to calm the fuck down! I can get you kicked out for touching me like that."

Her face and shoulders drop. "I'm sorry." She steps over to me again and wraps her arms around me. "It's just the thought of you and her—it drives me crazy."

A *little* bit of guilt hits me.

"This is my home," she cries. "Please don't say anything. I won't touch you like that again, I promise. The club is all I've got."

I rub her back. "Okay, okay, I won't." I hate it when women cry. "I've got stuff to do for the club. I've got to go on the computer."

She inches back, wiping away her tears. "Okay. You say nothing about me pushing you, and I won't say anything to Reaper about why his sister's earring was in your bed, because that discussion won't end well for you."

I move away from her, curling my lip in disgust. The audacity to threaten me. "Get out!"

She leaves.

I just got whiplash. Were those tears fake? That woman is crazy! How did I not see this before? A ripple rolls down my spine. All it would take is to piss her off and she'd snitch to Reaper. But is she willing to risk her life here if I tell the club she laid hands on me? I don't think I want to take that risk. I clench my hand. This is bullshit!

I go to my top cupboard and search through the back. Well, at least Mercedez didn't find Milly's underwear. I'm sure that would set her off even worse.

I head downstairs, looking for Milly. I spot Mercedez in

the lounge with the other sweet butts, watching TV. I look around but don't see Milly, so I go outside.

Milly's sitting at a table, watching Ava, Hope, Elena, and Ivy's little one, Sammy, playing on the playground. I walk up to her. She flashes me a sweet smile, and it hits me right in the chest. Fuck, she's beautiful. I take a seat. "We have a problem."

Her eyes bulge. "What's wrong?"

I put my hand out, showing her her earring. "Missing something?"

She grabs it. "Where did you find it? I've been looking everywhere."

"Mercedez found it," I say, cringing. "In my bed."

Milly's face falls. "She didn't?"

"Oh, she did, and she threatened to tell Reaper."

Milly looks away, blinking rapidly. I raise my hand to touch her cheek, but I force it back down. We can't have anyone suspecting anything. "Don't cry, pretty lady. All she's got is an earring from my room. We're friends. You could have been in there for a chat."

She swallows hard. "If Reaper asked me point-blank if I slept with you, I don't think I could lie to him."

I get that. I don't think I could lie to him either, even if telling the truth was to my detriment. "I'll make sure she keeps her mouth shut. I warned her I'd get her banned if she touches me again, so we have this deal where we keep each other's secrets."

Milly inches back, studying me. "What do you mean 'banned if she touched you *again*'? What did she do?" Her voice is hard.

"Wow! Remind me not to get on your bad side," I joke to lighten the mood.

Her lip twitches.

"Mercedez pushed me in the chest out of anger." It's better than a slap, I guess.

Milly shakes her head. "If she touches you again, tell me!"

Something tells me Milly might actually lay hands. She's not one to put up with shit, but it will cause a scene and everyone will want to find out why they're arguing. So I can't really tell her if it happens again. Still, it feels good she cares.

Milly's phone rings. She pulls it out of her pocket. "Milly speaking." A pause. "Yes, sure. I'll be right in." She looks at me, scoots out of the chair. "Work called me in again. There's sickness running rampant throughout the hospital, and we're short-staffed."

"You work too much." I never see her take part in a hobby or enjoy life.

She pauses. "Yes, I do."

"Go save some lives."

She gives me a genuine smile. "Can we talk about this more later?"

I nod. "Sure."

As I watch her leave, pride rises in my chest at her accomplishments. Her life at the hospital, dealing with life and death every day, must be so stressful. I can't imagine it, but she does an impressive job not bringing it home. Sometimes she's tired or quieter than normal, but most of the time she's smiling.

I frown. Am I going to be the reason she loses her only family? Am I selfish enough to keep this going? I don't think Reaper would disown her. I'd be the one punished. But I don't know for sure, and it's starting to eat at me. Still . . . I can't say no to Milly. Whatever she wants, she gets. She's my deadly obsession.

MILLY

MY HEAD IS SPINNING OUT OF CONTROL LIKE A CYCLONE. Mercedez knows . . . or at least suspects. Out of all the people who live in the clubhouse, she's in the top two I wouldn't want to know. Now she can manipulate us, and she's exactly that type of woman—the kind who'll do anything to get her own way. Two of her closest sweet butt friends who used to live in the clubhouse caused all sorts of trouble for Ava and bullied Elena. They say you are who you hang around with, and it's true.

I shove my bag into my locker, harsher than necessary.

"Are you all right?" a deep voice asks beside me. I turn to see a handsome man with thick gray hair, clean-shaven. The gray actually suits him.

I have to clear my throat to snap out of my little daydream. "Yes, I'm fine, thank you."

He gives me a friendly smile that lights up his face.

"Sorry, we haven't met. My name is Milly White. I'm an ER doctor here." I put my hand out, and he shakes it with a firm grip.

"Edward Stanley. *Lovely* to meet you, Milly. I'll be working beside you as an ER doctor."

I let out a sigh of relief. "Thank the Lord. I've been waiting for them to hire someone for some time now."

He chuckles. Our pagers beep. We glance at each other, then rush down the hall toward the ambulance bay, where two ambulances arrive with flashing lights. I head to the first, Edward to the other. I open the doors and look at the paramedic. "What do we have?" And so my day begins.

After the hectic morning, when I have ten minutes free, I grab a sandwich and sit at a table in the cafeteria. I'm prepared to have to leave at any minute, so I shovel the sandwich down like a starving animal.

I hear laughter as Ivy sits down across from me. "Do I have to do the Heimlich maneuver on you?"

I shake my head, grinning as I chew.

"How's that new doctor doing? I heard he's gorgeous," she purrs, fluttering her eyelashes.

I swallow. "Very good looking." Very much my type, but noooo, my thoughts are tangled up on a man I can never have a relationship with.

"There's a buzz around all the women. He's the most eligible bachelor at the hospital," she says.

My eyes widen. "How is *he* still single?" Jeez, they know more than I do, and I work with the guy. A gorgeous man like that would surely have a wife.

She leans across the table. "I heard he's divorced and came out here for a change."

Not surprising. Divorce rates are high for doctors. We work long hours, miss special events, and when duty calls, lives are on the line.

She looks at me curiously. "What's he like?"

I chuckle. "We haven't had any personal conversations. It's been busy, but he seems friendly with staff, families, and patients. He's thorough and experienced in his job, from what I've seen so far. We communicated well today, and he fits in with the team."

She giggles. "Oh, I bet he is fitting in *perfectly*," she says with a wink. "So, you know that doctor show . . . What's its name . . ." she clicks her fingers. "*Grey's Anatomy*."

I nod. Yes, it's a classic, and they still show it on streaming services.

"Well, the nurses started calling him McDaddy."

I laugh out loud. "That is hilarious. Whoever thought of that deserves a medal. He's a silver fox."

"How old do you think he is?" she asks.

I pause, thinking. "Maybe fifties." I shrug. "I'm terrible at guessing ages, so don't take my word for it."

She looks at her watch. "I've got to head back, but find out some gossip on McDaddy, will you? The nurses are dying to know."

"I'd better get back too. I can't make any promises—it's busy in there." My beeper goes off. "I'm coming," I mumble, standing up and rushing toward the ER.

By the time my shift is finished, I'm exhausted. My feet ache; my shoulders are tense. I get changed and sling my bag over my shoulder. Just then, McDaddy walks over, wrapped in a towel—fresh from the shower. I whirl away, but not before I see his six-pack and the water droplets trailing his skin. "I'll leave and give you your privacy," I stammer, cheeks pink.

He chuckles under his breath. "Are you working tomorrow?"

"Most likely," I answer, still focused on the door.

"Let's have a coffee. I'd like to get to know who I'll be working with."

"Sure, sounds great. Good night—" I almost said McDaddy. Ugh, damn Ivy for planting that name in my brain. "Good night, Edward."

"Good night, Milly."

Oh, that deep voice. Shit. I make my escape, ducking down the corridor, out the hospital, straight to the employee car park. I get in my car and drive back to the clubhouse. Once inside, I make a beeline for the kitchen to grab my trusty apple and spot Ivy and Sophie at the counter.

"Oh, she's home." Ivy claps with glee.

I look between the two of them. "You two look suspicious."

"Ivy was telling me about McDaddy." Sophie says his name salaciously.

I laugh. "There's not much to report, sorry."

They both whine.

"Between patients and paperwork, we didn't have free time. But I can confirm he has a six-pack."

They both squeal. "And how do you know this?" Ivy prods.

I click my tongue. "It was innocent. I was grabbing my bag, and he walked out of the shower in just a towel, so I left and gave him his privacy."

"Boo!" Sophie groans, giving me the thumbs-down. "You're no fun. That's when you stick around and say, 'Do you need help with that towel?'"

I giggle at her enthusiasm. "No, no, and no. Anyway, it was a hectic day. He's still learning, but he wants to meet for coffee tomorrow."

Sophie wiggles her eyebrows. "So it's a date?"

A loud thwack comes from the pantry. I peer around to see Twitch rubbing his head. He overheard us. I cringe.

"Are you okay?" I ask him.

He turns with a fake-ass smile on his face. "Yeah, sure. So tell me about this date you're going on tomorrow?" There's no mistaking the passive-aggressive tone.

"Yes," Ivy adds. "Fill us in."

"First, it's *not* a date. It's just two work colleagues having coffee."

Twitch gives me a look that suggests he doesn't believe me. I'm too tired for this conversation. I grab my apple. "I'm off to bed. Night, guys."

"Sureeeee," Sophie says, stretching the word, winking at me. "So when is this *date*?"

"The coffee catch-up," I stress, "will most likely be at lunch, *if* we actually get a lunch break."

"I want a full report on McDaddy after your next shift," Sophie calls out.

I snort at her. *"Good night."* I emphasize my words before going up the stairs and into my room, though with every step the guilt rises for saying yes to the coffee. It's just a meeting between colleagues. We'll be spending time together, so it's fair to say we need to get along. Trying to explain that to a jealous Twitch will be difficult. But do I even owe him an explanation? We aren't together, so why do I still feel so bad?

FIVE
MCDADDY

Milly

THE NEXT MORNING, I WAIT FOR MY LATTE BY THE COFFEE machine. I'm desperate for it. It wasn't nightmares that caused my dreadful night's sleep—it was a handsome, pierced biker with a sexy smile. I have an emotional hang-over, and I'm unable to stop the feelings I have for him. I hear footsteps and peer over to see the man himself walk into the kitchen. "Were your ears burning?" I mumble to myself.

He gives me a funny look. "What did you say?"

"Nothing," I quip.

He has a devilish grin. My pulse skyrockets as he stands directly in front of me, his hand grazing the skin between my shirt and pants. I frantically search around the kitchen. No one is there.

"What are you doing?" I whisper.

He leans down, and my breathing turns into panting. Just when I think he's going to kiss me, he grabs my latte, brings it to his lips, and takes a sip. "Thanks for this." Then the asswipe backs away.

I stand there, stunned for a moment. "Hey," I whine, "that was mine."

He shrugs. "Mine now. It tastes good."

"Yes, because *I* made it. You watch yourself, Twitch," I warn, and put my hands on my hips. "I know where you keep your secret chocolate stash."

His eyes just about pop out of his head.

"Yeah, that's right," I murmur, quite pleased with myself. That's where I'll be getting my snack tonight after work.

His hand comes toward me with the drink.

"Oh, no. You keep it now. You started this!"

His eyebrows pinch together—he's clearly unhappy that I threatened his precious chocolate. "When's your lunchtime? Is it about one?"

I nod. "Yes, why?"

"I was going to come have lunch with you." He looks away. "Oh, that's right. I can't. You've got a date with another man."

I smirk and lower my voice. "Are you jealous?"

He scoffs, and I laugh. "No, I'm not," he says defensively.

I point at him. "You so are!"

Ivy and Demon walk in, so I get to work making another damn latte. "Excited for your date?" Ivy asks.

I watch Demon raise a brow at Twitch. His lip quirks as if he's amused.

"It's *not* a date. He's my colleague. We'll be working together, so it makes sense we get to know each other and get along."

Ivy snorts. "You'll get along all right." She looks over at Twitch and cringes. "Morning, Twitch."

"Morning." His voice his dull, and he sounds unenthusiastic about this conversation.

I turn to Ivy. "I have to drive to the hospital. We're doing the same shift. Are you sure you don't want me to take you?" I peer at Demon. "Saves you a trip into town."

With a sharp shake of his head, he answers my question.

Ivy gives me a tight smile. "Thank you. My paranoid partner here"—she elbows Demon in the ribs—"is still insisting on taking me."

"That's okay. I wanted to double-check." I find it sweet that he still takes her to and from work. Even though the MC men are overprotective, it just shows that when they love, they love hard.

After my coffee is ready, I drink it while chatting with Ivy, then go upstairs, grab my bag, and wander back down to make my way to work.

As I pass by the computer room, someone grabs my arm and pulls me inside. The door bangs shut, my back up against it. Twitch leans into me. I'm breathing heavily, and the room feels like it's getting smaller. "What are you doing?" I ask quietly.

His body is firm against mine, and he rubs his hard-on against my groin. I whimper. His lips brush against mine, his breath fluttering against my face. He kisses the corner of my jaw, then lightly trails his tongue up to my ear, making me tremble. "I hope you remember this on your little *date*."

My mouth drops open. I grab his shoulders and push him off me. "You're evil!"

He laughs. I leave the room as quickly as humanly possible. I rush outside and to my car, where I attempt to get my breathing back to normal. He's making some risky moves in the clubhouse. Anyone could have seen us in the kitchen or him grabbing and pulling me into the computer room. I get a thrill from the teasing. It's addictive . . . or it will be until we get caught, that is. Together we are a firestorm, both intense and destructive, threatening to burn down our lives around us.

I get to work and head straight to the ER. Edward is already there, at the computer. I glance around. There don't seem to be any serious emergencies that aren't being attended to.

"Good morning," I say to Edward.

He looks up from the computer and gives me a lazy smile. "Morning."

"You're here early."

"Just trying to wrap my head around your computer system and seeing if I can help out."

I peer over at his screen. "Would you like any help?"

"Not for the moment. But I'm sure I'll be asking soon."

"No problem at all. Feel free to ask away."

"Are we still on for coffee?" he asks.

I smile. "Sure. I can have a chat with the most eligible bachelor in Crown Village Hospital."

He chuckles. "Is that what I am now? How do you know that?"

I glance at the three nurses staring at us, then lean in and whisper, "The nurses know everything."

He laughs again, and it makes me smile.

"Would you like to know your nickname?" I'm having way too much fun teasing him.

He cringes. "I'm not sure . . . Do I want to know?"

I give him a sharp nod. "It's a good one. I think you'll find it amusing."

He looks unsure. "Ahh . . . okay . . . shoot."

"McDaddy." I try to hide my laughter but fail miserably.

He looks stunned. "That's uh . . . interesting."

"Oh, come on, it's pretty funny."

He runs a hand through his hair. "Must be the gray hair. I'm not that old."

"How old are you?" It slipped out of my mouth before I could stop it.

"Late forties."

My eyebrows shoot up. That's not old at all. "Must be the gray hair." Plus the fact that he's ridiculously good looking.

"Get out!" a man yells. Our heads turn to a security officer pushing a guy out the door.

I rush to them with Edward by my side. "What's going on?"

"He was sitting with his friend over there," the officer says, glancing at the guy on the bed, who had overdosed. "He was stealing medical supplies out of the cabinet."

"You're a fucking liar!" the man spits. He pulls his arm back and punches the officer hard. The officer falls to the floor, blood gushing from his face.

Edward tackles the man while I kneel and tend to the officer. There's a cut above his eye that's bleeding.

"Are you all right to get up? You're going to need a couple of stitches." The officer sees the blood on his hand and faints, out cold. I sigh. "Can I get some help over here?" I yell. Nothing is ever dull around here.

The morning goes by quickly, with just a couple of minor workplace incidents and some teenagers being stupid with concrete. Yes, concrete. The stupidity of men will never cease to amaze me.

My stomach grumbles as I'm finishing up the paperwork. It's ten past one.

Edward leans in. "Ready for that coffee?"

I gulp. "Yes." I finish up on the computer, and we walk toward the exit. "Mary, are you okay here if we go grab a coffee for fifteen minutes?"

She looks between us and gives me a sly smirk. "Of course."

"Would you like me to grab you a coffee while I'm out?" I ask her.

"I'm all good, thanks."

As we walk down the corridor, Edward asks, "Is there anywhere in particular that sells the best coffee?"

I chuckle. "Sorry, you're out of luck. They're all average, but they do the job."

We wait in line at the closest indoor café. "So where are you from?" I ask.

"Reno."

When we reach the head of the line, the woman at the counter asks me, "What can I get for you?"

"I'll have a latte, with full-cream milk, thanks."

The lady gives me a small smile, and I pay.

"What's your name for the latte, so we can call it out when it's ready?"

"Milly," I answer, and then I go wait off to the side.

Once Edward orders, he waits next to me.

"There's a big hospital there. Why'd you move here?" We are still a decent-sized hospital, but we don't compare to the cities.

"I needed a change of scenery." He stares at me a little too long. "It was too suffocating there with my ex-wife."

"Didn't it end well?" I'm being nosy, but I'm curious.

He flinches. "No. It did not."

"Do you have kids?" I ask.

"My ex-wife and I never wanted them. Our careers came first."

I bob my head. "I understand that."

He focuses on me and leans forward. "Do you have kids?"

"No, and to be honest"—I glance away—"I don't know if I'll ever want them."

"When you have a career like ours, it's difficult to juggle everything," he adds, and I agree.

"Latte for Milly."

I step forward and grab my coffee. "Have a good day," the woman says.

I smile back. "You too."

"Flat white for Edward," she calls out next.

I step over to a four-seater table.

"Do you have a husband?" he asks.

I bring the hot mug to my lips and take a sip. "Certainly not." Even if I wanted to pursue one, I don't have the time.

He chuckles. "Why not? Someone as attractive and as smart as you, you'd have them lining up for you."

I snort loudly, and my cheeks flush with shame. "I guess when my life is work and my family is a bunch of bikers, meeting new people is difficult." Understatement of the year.

He coughs. "Bikers?"

Here we go. Every time I tell someone who my brother is, they all judge. "My brother is the president of the War Brothers Motorcycle Club here in Crown Village."

His eyes widen.

"Before you say anything and are quick to judge—they're not your typical motorcycle club. They help with the women and children's shelter here in town, and they are genuinely a good group of people." Unless you hurt any of them or the people they love.

His eyes are still wide. "Does your brother scare away your dates?"

Twitch's face is the first thing that pops into my head. "You could say that."

Someone joins us. I look up and see Twitch's face, and I stare, open-mouthed. I want to disappear. He has that sly, sexy smirk on his lips. He turns the chair around and straddles it and puts his hand out to greet Edward. They shake hands.

Edward gives me an odd look but returns Twitch's friendly smile.

I'm giving Twitch a death stare. I lay my hand on Twitch's arm. "What are you doing here?" I sound annoyed.

Twitch's eyes bounce between us. "Just thought I'd check up on how your *date* was going."

My breath catches. "Oh my god!" My cheeks are burning. I could wrap my hands around his neck and throttle him. "It's not a date." Well, I don't think it is.

"And you are?" Edward asks Twitch curiously, with no defensiveness in his tone.

Twitch, the sneaky devil, grabs my coffee and brings it to his lips and starts drinking it. That smug son of a bitch. Wait till I get home—I will devour his chocolate! He gives me a big grin, knowing he's taunting me. "The name's Twitch."

"That's a strange name."

All the MC men have weird names. Now I know the meaning of it, I reply. "It's because of his epilepsy."

Edward frowns. "Sorry to hear that."

"It's all good," Twitch replies. "Well, what are you guys talking about?"

I kick him under the table.

"Ouch!" He gives me a stern look.

"Don't you have somewhere to be?" I ask. Anywhere but here.

He shrugs. "No, I don't, actually."

This is not how I expected this coffee catch-up to go. My pager goes off. Saved by the bell.

"Have a good day Twitch, we have *work* to do." My tone might as well have said "go to hell."

"You have a good day too," Twitch says cheerfully, and I have the urge to stick my rude finger up at him.

"I forgot to give you back your panties that you left in my room. Maybe next time?" he says sheepishly.

I freeze, as if his words just tasered me. He's a nightmare of a person sometimes! My cheeks are on fire, and I briefly close my eyes, dying of embarrassment. I look around. Two nurses nearby heard him. I can tell from their giggles and whispers.

He sees the look on my face and walks out swiftly.

Yeah, you'd better run, punk! I swear he gets off tormenting me. I turn to Edward. "I'm so sorry about that. I never said it was a date."

He watches Twitch leave. "Are you two together?"

"No. He just likes to torment me." In every sense of the word. My pager sounds again. "Let's get going."

I dash back to the ER in a daze. The nerve Twitch has to show up and talk like that.

The day passes, and I'm struggling, eager to get home and give Twitch a piece of my mind. After my shift, I say my goodbyes to the team, but I'm awkward around Edward after I was embarrassed like that. I hope he doesn't think I'm lying and went around telling people it was a date. I cringe . . . *shame*!

Once I'm home, I'm pumped, ready to say what I'm really thinking, but I find Twitch at the bar—drunk.

I clench my jaw, but I smile at the ol' ladies and sweet butts watching TV. It must be a girly show because there are no men in there. There are MC men in the bar, playing pool and darts.

Twitch downs another shot. When his eyes meet mine, his lips curve up. "How was your date?" he yells out loudly over the top of everyone.

Everyone quiets. My hands tighten on my bag, like I imagine they would around his neck. I give him a psychotic smile. "It was no date." My voice is strained. "What part of that can't your small brain comprehend?"

Axle spits beer all over the pool table. Viper laughs out loud. Reaper walks over to me. Oh for God's sake!

"It was not a date," I repeat to Reaper, emphasizing each word.

"Do I need to do a background check on him?" Reaper asks firmly.

"Already did it!" Twitch calls out.

I roll my eyes. Of course he did. These men, I swear.

"I'm starving," I say to Reaper. I leave him to go to the kitchen, where I go straight to the pantry in search of that damn chocolate.

I move the flour, search around the cans, move the large bag of rice. *Score!* I grab two unopened bars. Even better. I open one, walk back to the bar, and just when Twitch makes eye contact, I take the biggest bite and moan loudly. "This is delicious."

He's glaring, and I swear he's foaming at the mouth. It makes my smile even wider.

"Where'd you get that from?" Cash asks from behind the bar.

I open my mouth to tell everyone about Twitch's little secret stash, but at the last moment decide against it. "It's mine. Sorry I can't share!"

Then I walk toward the stairs. I look over to see Twitch still staring while Mercedez strokes his arm. Then he lets her sit on his lap. The jealousy that scorches my chest is intense, stealing my breath. The taunt cuts deep. Is this payback for having lunch with Edward?

I grit my teeth but say, "Don't forget to take your tablets, Twitch. You should be aware alcohol can reduce the medication's effectiveness." Excessive alcohol can also trigger seizures. Even though he's made me angry, I still care about him.

I leave before I get a reply, storming up the stairs to my room. I grab my clothes and go for a shower. How natural it was for him to go back to the way things were before with Mercedez. I know he's been drinking, but it's easy to say no or to get her off him. My stomach knots, anger and hurt blooming in equal measures.

SIX
NEW YEAR'S

Milly

THE DAYS DRAG ON, EACH ONE BLENDING INTO THE NEXT AS I find myself stuck in a cycle of ignoring Twitch and throwing myself into work. It's easier that way—keeping busy, keeping my mind occupied. But no matter how hard I try, I can't stop thinking about him. Seeing Mercedez all over him that night hurt more than I care to admit. It was like a knife twisting in my chest, even though I have no right to feel that way. He's not mine, and I keep reminding myself of that.

Still, I've noticed she hasn't been sleeping in his bed. That small detail shouldn't matter, but it does. It gives me a sliver of hope I don't want to have. I have feelings for him—real, undeniable feelings—and I wish I could just turn them off. I wish I could shove them deep, deep, *deeep* down where they can't hurt me anymore. But I can't. No matter how hard I try, they keep bubbling to the surface, refusing to be ignored.

Today I can't hide behind work. I've been given New Year's Eve off, and while I should be grateful for the break, it leaves me with too much time to think. I offered to help in the kitchen, but the women waved me off, insisting they had it covered. Honestly, I don't blame them. Elena, Sophie, and I aren't exactly known for our culinary skills.

With nothing else to do, I decide to join Sophie at the gym. It's better than sitting around the clubhouse, stewing in my own thoughts. At least at the gym I can work out some of this pent-up frustration and maybe clear my head.

I'm huffing and sweating on the elliptical, looking like a drowned rat, while Sophie runs beside me, her glorious hair fluttering, hardly breaking a sweat. Some people are just blessed. I am not one of them. I wipe my sweaty forehead, slow down, and take a long drink from my water bottle, feeling immediately refreshed.

I'm on my feet all day during twelve-hour shifts, but fast-paced cardio makes me feel like I'm dying. "I can't do any more," I say through heavy breaths.

"Yes, you can," Sophie says encouragingly. "You've got this."

I step off the elliptical on unsteady legs. "No, I don't got *this* at all." My hands go above my head as I try to breathe in more air. "So what's happening tonight?" I haven't been to the clubhouse for New Year's because I usually work. I probably wouldn't have come anyway when none of the men had any ol' ladies and it was just them partying.

"Bomber got some fireworks, so that will be good. I'll be doing the shots and cocktails. Ava's in charge of the food. It'll just be music, dinner, and drinks." Her eyes narrow. "Twitch better let me choose some songs. The men always hog the music with their heavy metal."

I try not to laugh. I have no doubt Sophie will get her way. "I'll steal his phone for you if they don't let you choose a song."

She gives me a crooked grin. "I like how you're thinking. I can't believe I didn't think of that."

"Are you getting dressed up?" I ask.

She gives me a funny look.

Stupid question. "Of course you are." It's Sophie I'm talking to.

Sophie laughs, her eyes sparkling with mischief. "You should too. I know it's just us here, but sometimes it's nice to dress up for yourself. To feel beautiful, you know? It always gives me a confidence boost."

I raise an eyebrow, smirking. "You? Needing a confidence boost? Please. You're basically a Victoria's Secret model."

She grins, flipping her hair dramatically. "Oh, stop. But also, go on."

I laugh, shaking my head. "I'm serious. You're gorgeous, Sophie. You don't need a dress or makeup to feel confident."

"It's not about needing it. It's about doing something for yourself. When I take the time to dress up, even if it's just for me, it reminds me that I'm worth the effort. You should try it sometime."

Her words stick with me. Maybe she has a point. It's been a while since I've done something just for me—something that makes me feel good, confident, beautiful. After the kidnapping, I wasn't myself for a while. It was like I was in someone else's body, and I couldn't shake how on edge I felt, even though I knew I was safe and those men were dead. It's taken time, but I'm starting to feel like myself again. I guess when that kidnapper hinted that he was going to rape me, all I wanted to do was dress down and be unattractive. He made me feel dirty. Now that I'm getting my confidence back, maybe I should dress up.

"I'll give it a shot. But don't expect me to strut around like you do."

Sophie winks. "Oh, honey, no one can strut like me."

On my way to the shower, I see Zara. I give her a smile and a quick hug. "I'm so excited for you," I tell her, glancing down at her baby bump. "How are you doing? I feel like I've hardly had a chance to talk to you about it all."

"Thank you." She smiles brightly. "This pregnancy is really taking it out of me." She rubs her tummy, and it's the cutest thing. "I've been going to bed real early, and with the vomiting and still working the same hours at the shelter, it's been rough."

I put a hand on her arm. "I have one word for you: delegate. The shelter is a lot to manage, and you need to lean on your staff. Rest is important, my love, and you're going to need to get as much as possible before this beautiful baby comes."

She lets out a little sigh. "Bomber's been onto me about cutting my hours and relaxing more. It's just that I built that shelter from the ground up. The work we do for women and children is important. I'd hate for anything to fall through the cracks."

"I understand, but it's also important to manage your stress levels and get rest. Just try to lean on your staff. You might be surprised at how capable they are."

She nods. "Okay, I will."

"If you have any concerns about the baby, I'm always here for you, no matter what."

"Thank you. I do feel better knowing you're close by if I ever need help."

Happiness bursts inside my chest. I'd do anything for these women.

I shower, then scan my wardrobe. Being a simple woman, I choose a dark purple dress with a subtle floral pattern and long sleeves. I'll wear it with my boots. I style my hair in waves and add subtle makeup. The music downstairs grows louder, but I pause before going down. I'm not in the mood yet. I need a little me time. I borrowed one of Elena's romance books, so I lean back on the bed and begin to read.

Hours go by. It's so easy to get lost in a book. I must admit, I'm kind of jealous of how easy the main character's life is.

I decide to finally make an appearance and go downstairs. Sophie is behind the bar. When I reach the bottom of the stairs, our eyes meet. She lets out a dramatic sigh. "Finally, you're here. Now you need to catch up on drinks."

I chuckle and glance around. Everyone must be outside, so I go to the bar. "What have you got for me?"

She picks up two pink shots and puts them in front of me. "Two wet pussies," she purrs. "I put your piña colada in the fridge because I didn't know how long you'd be."

Her excitement makes me smile. I take one shot, then the second, feeling the burn of the alcohol and tasting a tinge of sweetness. I cough. "I don't mind that one."

"I bet you don't," she says, giggling. She's so sassy.

My phone pings with a message from Edward.

> I hope you have a great New Year with your family.

> Thank you! I hope you have a great New Year too!

"WHAT ARE YOU SMILING AT?" HER VOICE CARRIES ALL THE innuendo.

"Edward sent me a New Year's message, wishing me a good night."

She flutters her eyelashes. "How is McDaddy?"

I chuckle and think before I speak. "He's nice and professional."

"Nice . . ." She sputters. "Oh, please." She rolls her eyes. "At least you have someone hot to look at while you're at work."

True.

"Let's go outside. Everyone else is out there," she says.

"Did you get your song yet?" I ask.

She narrows her eyes. "Not yet."

"I'll go get his phone for you."

"Muwahaha," she says evilly.

We head out to the backyard, and I glance around until I see Twitch sitting at the table next to Axle and Viper. Sophie takes a seat next to Viper and gives him a chaste kiss on the lips.

"Twitch," I say.

He looks at me, and his heated eyes roam over me. Axle notices and elbows him in the ribs. Some men think Twitch has the hots for me, and Ivy said Axle teases him about it.

"Can you come and help me with the internet?" I ask. "My phone's not connecting properly."

"Yeah, sure," he replies with a wicked glint in his eyes.

Peeking over my shoulder, I see him watching my ass as I walk. When we go inside, he says. "Let me have a look at it for you?"

I look around. The kitchen and hallway are empty. I grab Twitch's arm and pull him around the corner. "I told a fib. I just wanted to talk to you."

He gives me a slow, seductive smile. "You want to talk to me now? Looks like you wanted nothing to do with me the past few days."

I bite my lip, unsure whether I want to tell him why. "Well, you and Mercedez were looking really close again, so I thought I'd keep my distance. I didn't want to disrupt whatever you *two* have got going on."

He laughs. "There's never anything going on between me and her." He cocks his head. "Were *you* jealous?"

"No," I'm quick to reply. "I thought I was doing the right thing." Was I jealous? Of course I was, but I'm not going to tell him that.

I take a step toward him until our bodies meet, and I feel the scorch of heat go straight through me. I reach up under his shirt, and I touch his hard abs. His body shakes and he sucks in a breath. I smile. My other hand goes to his jeans, and I slide it into his pocket. *Score*! I pull out his phone.

"What are you doing?" he asks, his voice husky.

I give him an innocent smile, shove the phone in his face to unlock it, and I bolt, running as fast as I can through the kitchen, out the door, and off toward Sophie. I hear heavy boots behind me, which just makes me giggle more.

"Hey," he says, his voice playful. "Give that back."

I laugh, thinking it's hilarious, and pass the phone off to Sophie. She holds on to it for dear life, and I rush to take a seat next to Ivy. The music changes to a techno beat, and Axle lets out a gigantic groan, narrowing his eyes at me. "Really, Milly? I thought we were friends."

I wave him off. "Let her choose a song."

Twitch shakes his head with a grin and takes a seat opposite me.

"Oh, damn," I say. "I forgot my drink."

Elena stands with her empty glass. "I'll get it for you. I need a glass of wine anyway."

"Thank you! It's the cocktail in the fridge."

She's so lovely.

I look around to see Sammy on the play equipment and Hope on the swing. Ava is pushing her. The sweet butts and a few of the men are sitting on sandstone blocks around the fire. It's relaxing out here, and with the trees and being on the edge of the national forest, it's a great spot.

After dinner, we all sit around the fire, drinking. Sophie and Cash plan on getting us all drunk, I'm sure of it, as the drinks just keep appearing. It's a happy vibe, full of talk and laughter. I get the evil eye from Mercedez every now and again, but it's nothing I can't handle.

Bomber and Demon coordinate the fireworks. They let off loud cracks, spiraling and shooting into the sky in vibrant splashes of color and unique designs. It's spectacular. I love seeing the huge smile on Sammy's face. The close bond Demon has formed with her is a beautiful sight. Demon and Bomber changed when the right women came along.

Is it possible that Twitch could see our relationship as more than just sexual tension? Could someone like him ever commit? I hear my brother's laugh and look across the flames to see Ava on his lap. The sight snaps me back to reality. It wouldn't matter if Twitch could see us in a relationship because it's never going to change the fact that my brother is the club president and we are defying him.

Ivy sits beside me. She frowns. "What's wrong?"

I fake a smile. "Nothing."

She leans close and lowers her voice. "Is it about who I think it is?"

I reluctantly nod.

"Do you want to go inside and talk?"

It must be the alcohol, but I'm feeling a little extra emotional tonight. "Okay."

As we're walking up to the house, Ivy says. "You look really beautiful tonight."

"Aww, thank you. Ever since the kidnapping, I've been down, but I'm starting to feel like myself again, so I thought I'd get out of the sweatpants and dress up."

Her brows pull in as she opens the back door for me. We step inside.

"So you're feeling better? That's great news! I know we've

talked about what we've gone through, but I always thought you were just saying it to make me feel better. You're always so put together and strong. No one would have ever known you were struggling."

We walk up the stairs toward the bedrooms.

"I was being honest. I'm good at hiding it. I'm surprised you haven't heard me cry out in my nightmares." Because Twitch is there, I'm lucky to feel safe, secure, and able to overcome my fears. Even though I like him as more than a friend, he's the friend I always wished I had.

"All the women seem to have gone through something traumatic, so I never would have guessed who it was, and it was none of my business, so I never asked."

I love that about the club ol' ladies. No one judges. It's refreshing. We all want what's best for each other. Well, all the women do, except for Mercedez. She looks out for number one only.

We go into my room and sit on the bed. "What's going on?" she asks, leaning forward to listen.

"It was supposed to be innocent fun, no strings attached, but I'm catching feelings, and I can't help it."

She gives me a look of sympathy. "I get it. I caught feelings early on with Jett. The MC men seem to have that effect on us."

I groan. "It's the heated looks, the secret touches, the teasing. When I'm with him, all thoughts of the consequences disappear, leaving only longing. Later I'm left with the weight of the guilt. But I can't seem to end whatever is going on between us, and he can't either. We're stuck, and I don't know what to do. There's no way this can work out well for us." Even though I was jealous that Mercedez was on his lap, I can't help but still want him, and I hate it. I should have more respect for myself, but I can't stop the way I feel about him.

She gives me a hug. "I can't imagine how difficult it must be for you. If only I had something positive to say."

"I'm not a one-night-stand type of girl, and this is why. I catch feelings," I chastise myself. "I should have anticipated this when we had sex." My stomach drops low. "I'm worried about what we have ending, but I'm also worried we'll get caught. My brother is my family. He's been everything to me, and he's the club president. Loyalty and rules are important to him. We either lose what we have, or we lose our relationships with my brother." Tears fall, and I feel stupid. "Don't mind my drunk talk."

She rubs my back soothingly. "Your feelings are valid. I'm sorry I have no helpful words of wisdom for you. I just want you to be happy, and I hate that you're in this position."

I wipe my tears. "Thank you. Well . . . I might get some sleep." I'm embarrassed about my outburst.

She nods, says good night, and closes the door behind her. I get changed, feeling rude for not saying good night to everyone outside, but I assume they're all drunk and won't notice I left. I snuggle into bed and let a few more tears fall, dampening my pillow, before I roll over and fall asleep.

The sound of the door opening wakes me. The light from the fire filters through the curtains, showing Twitch moving toward my bed. "What are you doing?" I ask sleepily.

"You've been gone for a while. I was just checking on you," he replies.

It makes me smile. "I've been working long shifts. I think I needed an early night." A half-truth.

The bed dips as he sits beside me.

"No one saw you come in, did they?" I ask.

"No, everyone's still outside drinking."

"I'm okay, so you can go out and celebrate with everyone, especially Mercedez." I didn't mean for my voice to sound so bitter, so I add, "Thanks for checking on me."

He leans down, looking at my lips. My heart races.

"I don't want her. I want you."

I hear everyone outside counting down. "Ten, nine, eight, seven, six . . ." My breath gets heavy. "Five, four . . ." The anticipation is cruel. "Three, two . . ." Instinctively, I raise my chin to meet his lips. "One." His mouth finds mine, soft at first, as if asking for permission. Then the kiss deepens and fire burns through me.

I reach up and tangle my fingers in his hair, eliciting a moan from him. The tip of his tongue flicks out to touch mine, and I angle my mouth. He sweeps his tongue against mine, and he tastes like mint. He inches back. My chest rises and falls as I try to catch my breath, my lips tingling from the intensity of the kiss. His forehead rests against mine, and I can feel the heat radiating off his skin. The arousal I feel for him is consuming, and I want him all over again.

"You're going to be the death of me," he murmurs, his voice low and gravelly.

I let out a shaky laugh. "Funny, I was about to say the same thing."

His lips curve into a wicked grin and he leans in, brushing his mouth against mine in a teasing, featherlight touch. "You have no idea what you do to me," he whispers, his breath warm against my lips.

I swallow hard, my heart pounding in my chest. "I think I have a pretty good idea."

"I had to come see you. I needed my New Year's kiss," he says huskily.

I'm overheating. I lick my lips, tasting the last remnant of him. "You got your kiss." The yearning in me demands that isn't enough. It can't be.

He chuckles, "Yeah, I did. But I want to kiss somewhere else."

Before I can say anything, he's pulled the blanket off and

is tugging down my pajama pants, making me chuckle. I glance at the door, torn between wanting his mouth on me and worrying about someone hearing us. He rips off my underwear and I shiver with excitement. Any thoughts of stopping him vanish.

"Open your legs for me," he murmurs in a deep, sexy voice.

I do as I'm told, and he moves between my legs, his hot breath tickling my skin. His sudden touch on my clit makes me hiss and buck. His thumb rubs circles over the nub, and my back arches and pleasure shoots through me.

He lets out a satisfied grunt, and his tongue laps at me. I bite back a moan, trying to be quiet when all I want to do is scream. He presses down with his hot tongue. Waves of heat crashes through me as he applies pressure, stroking in a steady rhythm. When he seals his mouth over my clit and sucks, I clench my teeth together as I ball a fistful of the bedsheet.

He buries his face, sucking and licking me harder. I squirm. The sensation is intense. I'm climbing higher and higher. He slips two fingers inside me and curls them against that special spot. A light sheen of sweat covers my skin, and my legs are trembling. His fingers keep rubbing and stroking. My eyes shut as sweet pleasure bursts from my core and I shatter. A soundless scream is on my lips as I ride out an intense orgasm. As I'm coming down, I feel a blanket being pulled over my legs.

"Hear me out. How about we spend tomorrow together?"

I give him a lazy smile. "You mean today," I joke.

He chuckles. "Yeah, today. Let's book a hotel out of town and spend some time together. Just you and me."

"I'd love that." I need it. Just us two. No fear of someone walking in. We can just be *us*. It's something I've craved since

I met him. We always clicked, but I've never gotten to spend quality one-on-one time with him.

He gives me an earth-shattering smile and plants a kiss on my forehead, making me melt.

"I'll book it and say I'm visiting my mom. You tell everyone you've got stuff to do at your house. I'll message you the address tomorrow. Check-in probably won't be until the afternoon."

"Sounds like a plan."

He gets off the bed, goes to the door, and peeks outside. "Good night," he says over his shoulder.

"Good night, Twitch," I reply, and close my eyes with a smile and drift back off to sleep.

SEVEN

STOLEN MOMENTS

Twitch

I'M CONVINCED MILLY'S A WITCH. SHE'S GOT ME UNDER HER spell, and I'm a goner. She could say the sky is bright pink and I'd agree with her with a smile on my face. I noticed she was off last night, and when she disappeared, I was on edge, checking the back door every ten minutes for her. She's my addiction, and I can't get enough. Being without her is like going through withdrawals—everything hurts.

She left for a few hours, and I couldn't concentrate while she was gone. The thought of her upset and alone was like a blow to the chest. I wonder . . . am I the reason she was upset? I shake my head. I'm so full of myself. She doesn't care about me that much. But I saw the jealousy in her eyes when she thought Mercedez and me were back to normal, which is laughable because we never will be.

Maybe I should pay more attention when Mercedez is touching me. Most of the time, I don't even realize she's sitting next to me. I'm used to her touching me, but it means nothing. It never did, but it affected Milly. So I must mean something to her. The thought alone makes me one very happy man—that she likes me more than I ever thought was possible.

The men in the MC have made it clear that she's out of my league, and I've always known it. It's one thing to sleep with her, but for her to give a shit about me is something else. I don't deserve it, but I'll take it. Just the thought of being worthy of her stirs something deep inside of me. But will Reaper let me live to see it through?

I'm standing against my bike, waiting for her so we can check in. Milly deserves the best, so I got a fancy place two towns over. I don't think I've ever spent this much money on a woman, but I went all out. It's a matter of time before she sees the truth. She's too good for me and will end whatever we've got going on. I need us to have this time together.

If only for one night, I can prove how good we could be without all the bullshit. But when tomorrow comes and we have to leave, I know what will happen. She'll choose her brother, and I'll choose the MC—the second family that gave me a chance and pulled me out of my depression. I think I could choose her over everything else, but with our limited time, it's not worth the risk of losing both the MC and her. Milly and Reaper are close. I wouldn't hold it against her if she chose him, but I can't lose everyone when she comes to her senses and realizes I'm not worth it.

I remember when I was a prospect and Milly arrived to talk to her brother. It was the first time I saw her, and I swear I stuttered just saying hi. She had an aura of friendliness and confidence, with a beautiful smile that lit up her face. I'd never been struck by someone's beauty before, and I'll never forget that day. It's burned into my brain.

Her silver convertible enters the parking lot, and she parks next to me. *So, this is fucking happening.* My heart hammers. She gets out of the car dressed in a long white dress. As usual, she's breathtaking. She could wear granny panties and have messy hair and I'd still get hard over her.

I can't stop smiling as I walk over. She beams at me. Once I reach her, I grab the back of her head and give her a hard kiss. I give her a once-over. "You look divine."

Her cheeks flush, and I love it. I don't think she realizes how beautiful she is.

"Well . . . hello to you too," she says giddily.

"For tonight and tomorrow morning, we're free to be together and be ourselves." I've wanted this day since the day we met. All the small moments together were never enough to satisfy my insatiable hunger for her.

"I know. I'm glad you suggested it."

Relief floods me. "Where are your bags? I'll grab them."

She opens the back door and pulls out a bag. I take it from her and grab my own from my bike, and we go to the front office. The building is enormous and overlooks a lake. I give my name, we sign in, grab our key, and go up in the elevator. I'm on a high. Milly's my dopamine. It's a comfortable silence as we smile at each other. The elevator pings, and we step out onto our floor.

She links her arm with mine as we walk to our room. I swipe the key card, and we head inside. The lights come on, revealing a neat, luxurious room with a king-size bed, a large TV, a fridge, and a sofa. It's small, but it's nice. It's all we need. I put our bags beside the bed.

"Is it up to your standards?" I ask, half joking, half serious.

"Of course it is. It looks great."

"They have a pool and a hot tub, and there's a massage

place downstairs too if you'd like to book in for tomorrow." I wanted to make this the best experience possible for her.

She gives me a friendly smile that reaches her eyes and sits on the bed. "I'm just happy to get away. I can't remember the last time I even had a holiday, so thank you for this."

I did something right, and I'm stoked about that. I take a seat beside her. "You need to enjoy yourself more, if you've never taken time away." I feel bad for her. She works herself to the bone but doesn't take time out for herself.

"I know. The hospital is always short-staffed, and I don't want to let them down," she shrugs. "And it's not like I have a family to go home to like some of the other doctors, so I always say yes to extra shifts."

I frown at that. "You have a family. You have the MC. Just because you don't have kids doesn't mean you're not entitled time off to enjoy yourself."

She puts her hand over mine. "You are kind. Thank you for reminding me. Life gets busy, and I'm used to putting my hand up to help the hospital when I can, but now that we have a new doctor helping, I'll be able to take more time for myself."

My top lip turns up at the thought of that doctor. McDaddy. What a shitty name.

Milly laughs. "You should see the look on your face. He's a nice guy."

"Who wants to get into your pants," I add. I'm not blind. I saw the look in his eyes.

"No, it's not like that." She's so sure of herself, but so naive.

"How many other people did he have one-on-one coffee dates with?" I ask with a raised brow.

She looks away.

"Yeah. None of them, I bet. I'm telling you—he wants you."

She rolls her eyes. "I disagree. We'll be working long hours together, so he was simply getting to know me."

I huff. "Keep telling yourself that. Anyway . . . enough about the doctor." I stand and put my hand out. "Let's go get something to eat."

She puts her hand in mine. I pull her to her feet and give her another kiss, but I pull back because I'm getting hard. "I could kiss you all night. Quick, we'd better go before I change my mind. Once we get comfortable, I won't want to leave this room until checkout."

She pauses like that sounds like a good idea to her. I pull her along, but she resists and giggles.

"Food first, then let me ravage your body."

MILLY

WHO CAN PROMISE TO WORSHIP MY BODY BUT THEN MAKE ME wait? I've been single for so long; if it weren't for Twitch, I'd probably be without sex another year. I step toward him until we're flush against each other. I snake my arms around his shoulders and stand on my toes to reach his lips. "I think we should get room service," I whisper. I bring my lips to his and then let out a shrill of surprise as his lips hungrily attack mine, reminding me he needs me as much as I need him.

He growls, and it's sexy. "I was trying to be a gentleman and take you out to dinner."

I smirk as his resolve fades. "I don't want a gentleman . . . I just want you." My heart leaps as he seizes my hips, drawing me closer. Our mouths find each other. He grasps my behind and hoists me up. I wrap my legs around his waist, our mouths staying connected. His arousal presses into me. Our tongues flick together, and a sultry noise escapes his throat, making me tremble.

I break away from his glorious mouth. "Twitch," I beg.

He strides toward the bed and gently lays me down while he settles on top of me. His lips travel down my throat, and his tongue flicks down every erogenous zone, making my eyes roll back. Open-mouthed kisses along my collarbone make me moan. He chuckles, so I open my eyes to see his smoldering gaze and devilish smile. He's enjoying this, taking his time, teasing me. Well, two can play that game.

I slip my hands under his club vest and tug on it. He gets off the bed, takes it off, and sets it gently on the table, like a prized possession. Thoughts of how important the club is to him flash through my mind, but I shake them away. I can feel guilty later. This night is about us, and I'm not going to let anything spoil it. It could be our last.

He takes a fistful of his shirt and yanks it off while I lift my dress over my head, letting it fall to the floor. His seductive grin as he stands there shirtless, his jeans hanging low on his hips, would make any woman drool. Heat rushes through me as he takes off his jeans and boxers. I awkwardly unhook my bra and kick off my underwear. My cheeks heat, and I'm suddenly insecure. I should have bought sexy lingerie, but the heat in Twitch's eyes shows that what I wear doesn't matter.

I stare at his dick as he strokes it. No wonder I was sore the next day. He's a beast—so big, and with metal pierced through the head. As he walks toward me, I swallow, stunned that this is real. We finally have our time together. I scoot up into the center of the bed. My breathing is out of control, and so is his. "Lie down," I say. "It's my turn."

His eyes darken and flare, but he does as he's told. I run my finger over his piercing and he bucks. I give his cock a quick squeeze; he's hard as steel. I move between his legs and lean down. My tongue darts out, tasting the head, and he moans, making me smirk. My eyes flutter closed as I suck him into my mouth. He hisses, and I take him as deep as I can. He's too big to take all of him, and I'm no pro, but I try my best.

"Fuck, Milly, just like that," he murmurs.

I'm soaking wet from pleasuring him. My mouth continues to work, sucking him deep and hard as his breathing gets more ragged. His hand tangles in my hair, controlling my movements, becoming more relentless, so I add my hand to the base and follow the rhythm.

"Milly," he growls. "I'm going to come."

He thrusts up and I take him deeper, all the way to the back of my throat.

"Ah, fuck!"

He comes with a violent intensity. I swallow every drop and lick him clean. He takes a moment. All I can hear is his heavy breathing. "You were made for me," he rasps.

I smile.

Then he sits up. "Now get your ass laying on the bed."

A delicious quiver travels through me. Once I lie down, his eyes drink me in, and the way he stares makes my insides coil.

"You're beautiful," he says, and it warms my chest.

The fire of anticipation courses through me. His expert fingers travel up my side to my breast. My body pulses with need as he caresses it, then drags his tongue between them, making me writhe under his touch. He brings his talented tongue to my nipple and traces circles around it. My back arches, a throb starting between my thighs as he gives the same attention to my other breast. I bury my fingers in his thick hair and tug.

"God . . . I need you," Twitch says huskily, making me whimper. I'm surprised he can go again so soon. Most men can't.

"But first . . ." he crawls down my body with eyes full of hunger and pushes my legs out wide before going to my aching core. I cry out as he sucks, strokes, and swirls the most sensitive part of me. He cherishes me, while all I can do is moan. I can't take it any longer. "Your tongue is amazing," I say between pants.

He inches back with a sly smirk. "My cock is better."

I melt. "Oh, please, Twitch. I need you inside me now." I need him more than I need to breathe. He leans over, opens his wallet, pulls out a condom, and sheathes himself. He crawls back up my body, taking his time with open-mouthed kisses that drive me crazy. I'm ready to come from the anticipation alone. He pauses and watches me.

One breath.

Two breaths.

Three breaths.

He leans down, and I wrap my legs around him. He drags his hard length through my core and presses it against my clit. I suck in a breath as he lines up at my entrance.

"I'm going to remind you who you belong to." His tone is possessive, and he thrusts in hard.

I gasp, seeing stars. Then he moves slowly and deeply. "Give me more," I beg. I need everything. He hooks one of my legs over his shoulder, then the other one. Pleasure rushes through me at the angle.

His head falls back, and he lets out a guttural groan, pounding into me while his thumb mercilessly rubs my clit. It's relentless. My moans grow louder. With skin slapping, he thrusts in and bottoms out. I want him to screw me forever.

His cock repeatedly hits my G-spot, and I clench around him. My nails dig into his fine ass.

"More," I cry out, and he gives me more. He fucks me. Sweat covers my skin. The bed frame keeps banging against the wall.

"You're so wet and perfect. I love your pussy."

I struggle to breathe. He pinches my clit and release bursts through my entire body. A life-altering moment of ecstasy travels through me. I know sex with someone else will never compare to this. His giant cock slams into me, and he lets out a long groan, his sounds of pleasure echoing throughout the room as the last wave of intensity washes over me.

He falls onto his back, and all that can be heard is our heavy breathing. I giggle. "I can see why Mercedez doesn't want to let you go."

He lets out a laugh, then rolls onto his side. "That was heaven. *You* are heaven."

I sigh. "It sure was." I could do it again . . . but my vagina and I need a break. But holy hell . . . it was hot.

His stomach growls.

I smirk. "We'd better get some room service. I know how precious you are about your food."

He nods, giving me an easy smile. "Good. I'm starved."

I get up, go to the bathroom, and grab two big, white, fluffy robes. I put one on and pass the other to him. I grab the menu from the table, and we browse through it, then call and order.

Once we finish our meal—the little pigs that we are—we also order chocolate cake for dessert. The whole time he's talking, he has chocolate on the side of his lip. I try not to crack up.

"What's so funny?" he asks.

I lean over and wipe off the chocolate with my thumb. "You're a messy eater."

He looks down at my vagina. "What can I say . . . I love my food." His tone, filled with sexual innuendo, makes me blush. I playfully whack him.

We lie in bed, and I snuggle into his side. The smell of sex and his cologne is heady, making me smile. My senses are drenched in him.

He turns on the TV. "Any requests?"

I yawn. "I don't mind." Twitch is good like that. While some of the men will turn their noses up and like watching only suspense or action movies, Twitch will gladly sit and watch anything. I love his easygoing nature. I could put on a crappy reality show, and he'd happily get invested in it.

If we didn't have feelings for each other and I lived at the clubhouse, we could easily be best friends. We get along so well, and it's hard to meet people like that anymore. With that thought and the warmth of his body, I succumb to the heaviness of sleep.

The sound of a phone beeping wakes me. The room is dark. I'm still in Twitch's arms. The light is coming from my bag. I lean over, grab my phone, and bring it to my face. The bright light makes me squint, and Twitch stirs beside me.

It's a message from Sophie on Facebook Messenger. It's a group message with all the ol' ladies.

> Hey bitches, I've organized for us to have a spa day at my family's hotel. I better see all of your beautiful faces there for some relaxation and champagne. It's booked for 11.00 a.m. See you tomorrow XOXO

"That's so bright," Twitch says huskily.

"Oh, sorry," I say, leaning over to put my phone on the bedside table. "I have to be back in Crown Village by eleven. Sophie organized a spa day."

He sighs. "Checkout is at ten, so that's fine." He pulls me

close and kisses the top of my head, making my heart clench. "Can we just stay here forever?"

I can hear the playfulness in his voice, but there's an undertone of sadness. I wrap an arm around him and give him a tight hug. "I wish."

He climbs on top of me. "Let's not talk about it." He leans down, kisses me, and once more ravishes my body.

EIGHT
REALITY SUCKS!

Milly

I FELL BACK ASLEEP, BUT THE EARLY MORNING SUN BEAMING through the sheer curtains wakes me. As the sun rises, so does the dread of having to leave. My mind races with thoughts of him saying, "I'm going to remind you who you belong to." It was hot coming from his lips, but what does that mean exactly? I overthink things too much. He was probably talking about sex, but there's this nagging sensation that last night was more than just casual sex.

His breathing changes, and he shifts. I can tell he's awake. I snuggle into him, finding contentment in the moment before everything has to change, before we have to return to the reality of our situation.

"Good morning, pretty lady."

"Good morning. How are you feeling?" My nerves coil as I wait for his answer.

"Like I had the best fucking night of my life."

I grin from ear to ear as the anxiety melts away.

"How are you feeling?" he asks curiously.

"Sore," I answer honestly. Because, well, I am tender this morning.

He rolls onto his side, his eyebrows pinched. "Did I hurt you?"

"No . . . well, yes, but in a good way. I'm not used to someone your size."

He gives me a sly smirk, clearly pleased with my response. "I want to wake up like this every morning." He leans over and squeezes my boob playfully. "With you naked in my arms."

I giggle, but pull the blanket up, feeling exposed.

He scoffs and pouts. "I'm obsessed with your body. Leave the blanket down."

I love how he always puts my mind at ease when I feel uncomfortable or self-conscious.

"Well . . . since you're sore, do you have any requests on what you'd like to do before we have to leave . . . outside of the bedroom?"

A thought comes to mind. "Yes, I do, actually."

He waits for my answer.

"I've always wanted to learn how to ride a motorcycle," I admit shyly. "But I never had the confidence to ask my brother. I understand if you say no," I'm quick to add. I don't want to make him feel bad, and I know how much their motorcycles mean to them.

He smiles indecently. "You're going to look sexy as fuck riding my bike." There was no hesitation; he obviously trusts me.

"Aren't you worried I'm going to scratch it?"

"That's what we have Axle for. He can fix it." He sits up in bed. "Let's go. You're going to love it."

We get changed. He insists I wear jeans and a jacket for safety.

As we head to the bottom floor, my heart races. We pass the receptionist and step outside to his bike. It's black with high chrome ape hangers and chrome wheels. I'm giddy as I stand beside it. I've wanted to learn how to ride ever since I saw my brother on one.

He helps me ease the helmet over my head and fastens up the strap under my chin. "Are you ready?" he asks coyly.

I nod, though my pulse is rapid. He helps me onto the bike, and I swing my leg over.

"Put the stand up and hold the bike up."

I swallow down some fake confidence and do as I'm told.

"First, check that the bike's in neutral by clicking the gear lever all the way down, then half a click up. Then turn it on." He points to the switch. "Press the button to start it."

I follow his instructions, and the bike roars to life. I jump. The exhaust is so loud.

"The front brake is on the handlebars, and the rear brake is on the right foot pedal. Next, pull the clutch in—it's on the left-hand side. Push the gear lever down with your left foot until it clicks. That's first gear. Slowly let the clutch out while giving it a *little* bit of throttle. But once you're moving, put your feet on the pegs. Go slow."

The bike moves forward as my grin stretches wide. "I'm doing it!"

He walks beside me as I go. "The safest way to stop is using the back brake. As you come to a stop, pull the clutch in and put your foot on the brake."

I do it, and the bike comes to a stop.

"You can do a small lap around. Just turn the handlebars when you want to turn."

I move forward again slowly, elated. I ride around the parking lot and stop when I see a car approaching. Even though I'm going slowly, I'm thrilled I'm doing it. I do three more laps before pulling the bike into its original parking spot. I turn it off, put the stand down, and once the bike balances, I jump off and straight into Twitch's arms. I laugh as he swings me around in a circle.

"You did great. Did you like it?" he asks enthusiastically.

"I loved it." I curl my fingers into his leather jacket and look up into those adoring eyes. "Thank you so much. I've wanted to learn to ride for so long, and I finally did it. *You* did that. *You* made it happen."

He pulls me into his chest, his biceps curling around me. "You're more than welcome. I'm stoked to see you so happy."

My eyes blur with unshed tears. He makes me feel like I'm his, even though I'm not. "I needed this time with you. Something as small as a getaway and teaching me to ride your bike. It means a lot." Being a doctor, I'm always the person helping others. I've never had someone who is genuinely happy just making me happy. We're like a jigsaw puzzle; when we're together, it feels like we're meant to be.

I snuggle into his shirt. "I don't want to go back," I whisper. Here in our little bubble, I'm happy, but why does it have to come with a price? Why do I have to have feelings for a man I'm not supposed to date?

He cups my chin in his hand and lifts my face to meet his gaze. His eyes swirl with a mix of emotions that reflect my own. He leans down and kisses me on the lips. The kiss is tender, and he holds on longer than normal.

"I want to stay too . . . but we can't." His voice softens at the end.

Dread cuts to the bone. I clear my throat. "I know." This short bit of time we've granted each other is going to make going home so much worse. I can't jump into his arms again. We can't kiss or have sex. He gives me one more quick peck on the lips, and we linger in each other's arms before we walk back to our room in silence, holding hands.

We pack our bags and leave, but my chest aches with a

new pain—a realization of what we can never have. Tears fall while I'm driving to the day spa.

I park outside, debating whether to go in. I don't want to disappoint Sophie. She's trying to do something nice, getting us all out to relax together. I take a deep breath, trying to organize my thoughts and emotions. I look in the mirror, run my fingers through my hair, and wipe my eyes. When I step out, Sophie is standing by the front door with a hand on her hip. I fake a smile.

She gives me a pointed stare. "I didn't think you were going to get out of the car."

Me neither. "No, I was coming in."

"You're the last one. The rest of the girls are up in the spa."

Once I get close to her, she grasps my arms and frowns. "What's wrong?" she asks with concern.

Oh, damn it. "Nothing."

"Bullshit!" she calls me out.

I chuckle, but it's flat.

"Are you crying over a man? Is it McDaddy?" she asks, her face twisting into a funny expression.

"No, it's not McDaddy."

"So it *is* a guy . . . Just because they're good for your hole doesn't mean they're good for your soul."

I burst out laughing. It's exactly what I needed. "True that."

"Come on, let's go get you a facial, a massage, a blowout, nails . . . the whole works."

I've never been a real girly girl. I've never been to a spa. Occasionally I get my eyebrows waxed, but that's my limit for beauty treatments. Still, a facial and massage sound heavenly.

Once inside the spa, I'm ushered into a room, where I get into a robe. I say hello to everyone and take a seat beside Ivy and Zara.

"Put your feet in the water. We're getting pedicures," says Ivy.

The water is warm and contains rose petals. Sophie comes to my side with a glass of champagne. I was going to sip it, but screw it—I down the lot. I feel all eyes on me.

Sophie laughs. "My girl's thirsty. Don't worry, I'll get you another one."

Ivy leans in close to me while everyone goes back to their conversations. "Are you okay?" she asks quietly.

I shake my head and lower my voice. "I spent the night with . . ."

Her eyes light up, but once she sees my sadness, she asks, "What happened?"

"It was amazing." Too good. Damn him and his rock-hard body! "Coming back to reality really sucks!"

"Oh." She sighs and squeezes my hand. "What's going to happen now? Does it change anything?"

I frown. "No, it won't." I take my new glass of champagne and sip it.

A phone rings. Sophie grabs it from her bag, answers, and lets out a long groan. "I told you already, there are female massage therapists here. I don't understand how many times we have to go through this. So go tell those jealous men of ours that there are no men here."

A few of us giggle at that.

"Okay . . . okay. Love you, bye."

I glance at Zara. "Have you been feeling any better?"

"Unfortunately, no, and I've been getting these bad headaches. I'm just stressing out that something's wrong."

"It's normal to feel that way, but maybe you should get a checkup."

She sucks in a breath. "Do you think something's wrong?"

"You should just put your mind at ease. Your doctor might give you something for the nausea and vomiting too."

She gives me a tight nod. "Thanks. I'll call to organize an appointment. I hope they can fit me in."

"Don't panic," I emphasize, but I see it does nothing to ease her.

She reaches over and grabs her phone. "I'll be right back."

My stomach drops. I've made her nervous. But she's better off getting checked out. I hope it's nothing, but I've seen so many pregnant women turning up at the ER with problems that should have been addressed earlier but weren't.

When she returns, she sinks back into her seat. "I've got an appointment later this afternoon."

I give her a small smile. "Wonderful to hear. Are you finding out what sex the baby is?"

"We decided not to. I'd love a surprise. My niece wants me to have a girl, but both Bomber and I don't mind. I just hope the baby's healthy."

When it's Elena's and my turn to have a facial, we lie down on the beds. "We are going to clean your faces first, using a gentle cleanser." The cleanser cools my skin. After rinsing, the esthetician applies a light product and begins massaging my face and neck. Elena moans, while I snort, then we are both left laughing.

When I return to the clubhouse, I feel relaxed. My nails look fresh from the manicure and pedicure, and I feel rejuvenated. I need to spend more time doing stuff like that, especially the massage. It's done wonders. Now all I want to do is sleep.

Everyone's gathered around the large dining table for dinner. It's awkward with me on one side of Twitch and Mercedez on the other, though when Twitch gives me a goofy smile while eating his meal, I smile back.

"I'm glad you're back," Reaper says to me. He's sitting at the head of the table.

"Were you worried I wasn't coming back to the club-house?" I tease.

"I wasn't sure, but"—he lowers his voice—"I enjoy having you here." He's a big, tough biker and the president of the War Brothers MC, but he's also a softy. It makes me wonder: If Reaper sees me happy with Twitch, would it be enough for him to let go of any resentment he has toward us? I'm worried he might carry some, given we're going against his wishes.

"Aww, well, I like staying here too and . . . I think I'll stick around for a while if you don't mind."

I hear someone coughing loudly, and I don't have to look to know it's Mercedez.

Ava claps with glee. "We would love you to stay here."

"Yes," Reaper adds. "That room can be yours. I'll run it by the club in the next meeting, but I can't see it being a problem."

My heart could burst with happiness. I didn't realize how much I felt like I belonged here. It seems more like home than my house does.

"So what did you get up to while you were away?" Mercedez asks with a fake smile.

My body tenses and Twitch clears his throat, but I look at her and give her a smile. "Not much, just some housework and watched some movies."

She gives me a dead stare, and my heart races. Does she know something? Is that the reason for the question? But no one knew about the arrangement to go there apart from me and Twitch.

"How's your family?" Ava asks Twitch.

He wipes his mouth. "Yeah, good." He looks away. "Everyone's good."

Oh, jeez . . . he's a terrible liar. When I dare take a peek, my brother gives him a funny look. I've been able to fake a smile my whole life, pretending everything's always good, but Twitch can't lie to save his life.

I yawn. "I'm off to bed. Those spa treatments have made me so sleepy." I stand.

"Are you working tomorrow?" Ava asks.

"Yes, I am. Have a good night, everyone." And with a round of byes I take my plate and put it in the dishwasher and go upstairs to bed, where mixed emotions about how I feel about Twitch and what we're going to do wreak havoc on my psyche.

NINE
GUILTY CONFESSIONS

Milly

I WAKE UP, GET CHANGED, AND GO DOWNSTAIRS, WHERE THE smell of toasted bread greets me. Demon is watching cartoons with Sammy and is braiding her hair. I let out a long, dreamy sigh, drawing Demon's attention to me. I walk toward them. "You guys are up early."

"Sammy couldn't sleep, so we came down here to watch some TV so we don't wake Ivy."

Aww, my heart. He's this big teddy bear when it comes to Sammy and Ivy, and it's the sweetest thing to see a violent, protective man find love and treat a woman like a queen. A tinge of jealousy hits me. I wish I had that.

"Well, have a good day, you two."

"Bye, Milly," Sammy says with a smile. She looks exactly like her mother, but with freckles.

At work, I put my things away and then go to the ER. Edward is with a patient. The nurse who's with him stares at him with a dreamy expression. The patient does too. She's around his age. She puts her hand on his arm and flutters her eyelashes at him. He's *very* popular around here.

The nurse running the ER announces, "There's a trauma case coming in with a gunshot wound to the chest. ETA five minutes."

"I've got it," I reply, dashing outside toward the ambulance bay while putting on my gloves. Adrenaline pumps through my veins as I wait.

Edward meets me outside. "I thought you might need a hand."

"You looked like you were needed inside," I say with a cheeky smirk.

He huffs. "She thought she was having a heart attack. I did a physical and a scan. It all looks fine. I'm waiting for the blood tests. By the sounds of it, I think she had a lot of caffeine this morning and she panicked."

"I bet she was over the moon getting you as her doctor," I joke.

He shakes his head with a grin. His eyes crinkle at the corners.

The sirens get louder until the ambulance comes into view. Once it reverses, the back doors open and a paramedic pulls the victim out. "Dorothy Anders, seventy-five years of age, one gunshot wound to the chest. She was in her home when a stray bullet hit her. There's no exit wound."

Dorothy keeps opening and closing her eyes, looking disoriented. Her distraught husband, pale and shaky, is by her side.

"She's incoherent, has a rapid heart rate, low blood pressure, shortness of breath, and swelling at the site," the paramedic adds.

The gunshot wound could have pierced her heart. We wheel her inside on a stretcher while Edward keeps pressure on the wound.

"Bay 2," the head nurse calls out, so we take her there.

Two nurses have the room set up, and we all move the patient to the bed so the paramedic can take the stretcher away

"Oh, Dorothy," the husband cries. "You have to save her," he pleads, looking at me. He grabs her hand. "She's all I've got. You have to save her!"

"We will do our best, Mr. Anders," I assure him, then look at the nurse. "Can you get him out of here?"

She nods and tries to pull him along, but he won't budge. "Come on, we have to let the doctors work on her."

"I can't leave her! She needs me!" His voice echoes with a haunting pain, but I focus on Dorothy. We roll her and double-check there's no exit wound, and then check her pulse.

"Weak pulse," I say to Edward, and he gives me a dire look. We take a scan of her heart to confirm it is what we think. We can see internal bleeding. It's catastrophic.

The husband is still screaming.

"Get him out of here!" I yell at the nurse, trying to concentrate. Another nurse comes over and helps move him out of the room.

Dorothy loses consciousness and becomes unresponsive. "Dorothy, stay with us," I say, but she flatlines. The long, eerie tone of the heart-rate monitor fills the room.

I start CPR. I'm puffing and calling out each chest compression as I go. I step away and look at the monitor, but it flatlines again.

"I'll do it," Edward says, leaning over Dorothy to perform the chest compressions. I'm catching my breath, watching him.

"Come on, Dorothy," I mumble.

After two more rounds of CPR, I call the time of death. I take off my gloves, and Edward and I walk out.

With each step, the dread of having to talk to Dorothy's husband builds. "I can talk to her husband, if you'd like," Edward suggests.

This was my patient. Unfortunately, it comes with the job; with the highs of saving patients, there are also the lows of them passing away. "It's okay." I give him a sad smile. "Thanks for offering." I make my way to the ER waiting room, and the husband spots me immediately and rushes over.

"What happened? Is she okay? When can I see her?" His eyes are red from crying, his voice is hoarse, and my chest aches for him.

"Let's go to a room and talk somewhere more private."

He shakes his head abruptly. "No! Tell me now!" he shouts, and I feel the eyes of the onlookers.

"I'm so sorry." I gulp. "The bullet pierced Dorothy's heart, causing extensive internal bleeding. She succumbed to her injuries. We did everything we could, but she died."

He drops to his knees, hyperventilating.

"Nurse!" I call out for assistance. I kneel by him, but he pushes me and I land on my butt.

"You killed her!" he screams, pointing at me with fury in his eyes. "It was you! You killed her!"

Two nurses rush to his side, so I stand, not wanting to upset him further by staying. His wife's injuries were too extensive—there was nothing more we could do.

"I'm so sorry for your loss," I tell him before I take a deep breath and walk away.

Everyone's eyes are on me, so I take a quick break and go outside, to the front of the building. As I dash out the front doors, the breeze greets my face and I can breathe again. Even though I'm somewhat desensitized to the grief of others, there are cases that still affect me. It comes with the job. You'd have to be a psychopath not to ever care.

TWITCH

I'M WEIRDED OUT. I GOT HOME YESTERDAY AND MERCEDEZ wasn't there. She's *always* there. I can't remember a time she left the clubhouse. I didn't ask anyone because I didn't want them to think I cared, and I don't, but I thought it was odd. Later that afternoon she returned, and even though we have no sort of relationship, I felt off-kilter. I need to get my shit together and sort everything out with her. I don't want to lead her on, but I also don't want to be a dickhead. And now, with her finding Milly's earring, she's only more suspicious, and I don't want her to cause problems or go to Reaper.

I'm going to have to have another firm conversation with her. I need to make it clear we will never be together. My head falls back in dread of epic proportions. I'm hoping she'll take it well, because even if she tells someone, who's going to believe her over me and Milly? Still, it's what needs to be done. I don't want Milly to think I'm playing with her and our time together meant nothing—because that's far from the truth.

Mercedez sat by me at dinner, but I ended up having an early night. She seemed off. I couldn't quite put my finger on it, but she wasn't as clingy as usual. Which I should be happy about, but I'm still on edge.

"Twitch, it's your turn, man," says Cash at the dartboard.

I blink a few times, snapping out of my daydream, and take a shot. I miss, and the dart bounces onto the floor.

Cash laughs. "It's not your day today."

A puff of air escapes my lips. "No, it's not."

He takes a step toward me. "What did you say to Mercedez? She's pissed off."

I glance over to see her in the lounge, glaring daggers at me. Cringing, I shrug it off. "I wouldn't know . . . probably just breathed."

He laughs. "Nah, I haven't seen her look like that before . . . like she wants to take your head off."

I freeze. Does she know? She couldn't. Milly and I didn't tell anyone, and we left separately. "God knows."

"Keep one eye open tonight," he whispers, and laughs.

"Oh, real funny!" I say, taking another peek at Mercedez. She's still glaring. I don't remember being an asshole to her, so I'm still at a loss as to why she's so angry. She gets up from the couch and strides over. I groan under my breath. Cash laughs again, thoroughly enjoying this. Oh, well . . . I'd better get this over and done with.

She puts her hands on her hips. "We need to talk."

I give her a sharp nod. "Yes, we do."

She glances at Cash, who turns away, pretending he's not listening.

"Maybe somewhere quieter?" she suggests.

"Okay, let's go to my room." I walk up the stairs and through to my room, where I close the door behind us. As I turn, a sudden sharp pain stings my face. The sound of a slap echoes. I touch my stinging cheek.

"You fucking asshole!" she yells.

I take a step away from her, blinking. "You hit me!" It's all I can say, because I'm still in shock. I lower my voice because others might hear us. "What the hell?"

She straightens her back and death stares me, eyes full of hatred. "You cheated on me . . . you slept with *her*, didn't you?"

"Are you fucking kidding me? Me and you aren't

together, and that is none of your business," I hiss. I should have denied it, but it slipped out.

She steps toward me and pushes me in the chest. I grab both her hands, holding her at a distance. She's fighting me and yelling. My heart races as I try to hold her securely without hurting her. I don't want to be hit again.

"You need to calm down!" My voice is harsh but firm.

She freezes, and her hands fall to her sides, so I cautiously let go, unsure of what's going to happen next.

"I was always there for you, and you chose her!" she cries, her voice breaking.

I calm my breathing. "I didn't choose anyone." Yes, I did, but she doesn't need to know that right now.

Mercedez pulls her phone from her pocket, activates the screen, and then pushes it in my face. It's a picture of Milly and me outside the hotel, kissing. My stomach drops. I move the phone out of my face and narrow my eyes at her. "You followed me?"

"Yes, so what? I put a tracker on your motorcycle. You were with her! What does she have that I don't?" Her voice sounds more hurt than angry now, and it makes me feel like shit.

My body stiffens. I pause, unable to find my words. She saw us kissing, and she has proof. I can't lie this time, and what if she goes to Reaper with the message? It could blow everything up. Caution is needed here. I gulp. "I don't know what you want me to say." I rub the back of my neck. "Me and Milly aren't together—we just spent the night together."

"Milly said she wanted to live here for good. She said it last night. Why would she stay if she thought nothing was going on between you two?"

Now I remember Mercedez asking Milly last night what she got up to. I should have caught on then. "But I don't know what's going on between me and Milly. We just slept together." Do I want something more . . . I don't think it's in our future.

Mercedez takes a deep breath and pulls out a pocketknife.

My heart is pounding and my breath is frantic. "Give me the knife, Mercedez," I say in a gentle tone.

She shakes her head; tears roll down her cheeks. The sharp blade flies out of the handle.

I'm sweating, but anxious and on guard. I'm unsure whether she's going to stab me or hurt herself. Fuck it. I can't live with myself if she hurts herself. "Mercedez," I say and take a step toward her.

More tears fall. The hand holding the knife trembles. "If you choose her over me, I'm going to kill myself." Her voice is filled with conviction, and I believe she'd do it. She's unstable. "The club is my only family. You're the only man I've ever loved. I can't lose it all."

Fear has me in a chokehold, but I make the decision. I rush toward her. She squeals and holds the knife up and away from me, but I overpower her. I grab the handle from her clutches and toss it away from us, onto the bed.

I wrap my arms around her, holding her as she cries hysterically and goes limp in my embrace. "Help!" I yell out. "Is anyone there? I need help."

After a moment, Ava rushes in, her eyes wide as her hand flies to her mouth.

"Go get Reaper and call an ambulance," I tell her.

She nods and leaves while I hold Mercedez, rubbing soothing circles on her back. "Shhh . . . it's going to be okay."

"But you chose her," she whispers, her voice cracking.

"I haven't chosen anyone," I lie. I'll always choose Milly, but I don't want to make Mercedez's condition worse.

I hear heavy footsteps. Reaper and Bomber stride into the room and approach us cautiously. Their eyes dart to the knife on the bed, then to Mercedez in my arms. The room feels claustrophobic as I feel the weight of their judgement. I try to step toward them to talk in private, but Mercedez grips my shirt. My mouth is dry as I struggle to find the right words without giving Milly's and my secret away.

"What the hell is going on here?" Reaper demands, his voice low and dangerous.

"She's not well," I say, nodding toward the knife. "She needs help. I think I should go with her to the hospital."

"No, not to *her*," says Mercedez, with a bite in her tone.

I suck in a breath as Reaper gives me an odd look.

"I'll be with you the whole time Mercedez. I'll stay with you for as long as I can, I promise." I'm quietly begging her not to say anything.

She pulls away and stares into my eyes. "You promise?"

I nod.

Her breathing stutters. "Oh-kay. If you leave me, I have nothing left."

"You need to go to the hospital," Reaper says in a softer voice as he talks to Mercedez. "We'll get you the help you need. We take care of our own."

She nods and her shoulders sag.

I stay with Mercedez. It feels like forever until the ambulance arrives, but once I hear the sirens and see those blue and red lights flashing through the window, I pick Mercedez up and carry her past Reaper and Bomber, downstairs and outside. Everyone's curious eyes are on us.

Trixie and Dolly dart over. "Oh my god, is she okay?" Dolly asks.

"She will be," I reply.

Once the ambulance pulls up outside the clubhouse, the paramedic gets out and asks questions, and I answer her while staring at Mercedez on the stretcher.

"Twitch," Mercedez calls out, stretching her hand to touch mine.

"You can come to the hospital," says the paramedic, so I jump up into the ambulance, take a seat, and take Mercedez's hand in mine.

"It's going to be okay," I say to her.

"I'll be okay if *you're* with me," she answers, and my gut drops to my feet. I may not see her as my life partner, but we have been friendly for many years now, and I'd hate to see her hurt herself because of me.

The paramedic fusses over Mercedez as I sit back and let her do her job. I space out on the way to the hospital. Dread builds when we reach it. The door opens and I see Milly's face.

"No!" Mercedez screams. "He's mine . . . Did you hear me, bitch? He's mine, not yours!"

Milly's face turns ashen.

"Milly, go and get the other doctor," I tell her. I don't want to make this situation worse.

She blinks a few times and dashes away while the ambulance crew brings the stretcher to the ground. The male doctor the women all love strides to us, then he's talking to Mercedez and the paramedic. Milly pulls me by the arm when we step inside the ER, but Mercedez screams out for me.

With a frown, I shake my head at Milly. "I can't do this right now. I must be with Mercedez."

"I'm sorry—you have to wait in the waiting room while we assess her," Milly replies.

My shoulders drop. "Just let me talk to her first."

I walk to Mercedez. "The doctor needs to talk to you. I'll be in the waiting room. I'm not leaving here, okay?"

Mercedez starts crying again, and as I walk out, she calls out my name. I flinch, but I keep on walking.

Milly ushers me out to the waiting room, where I plonk down on a seat.

"What happened?" she asks, concerned. "She tried to kill herself. Why?"

I raise my head. "She put a tracker on my bike, and she followed me. She has photos of us kissing outside the hotel." I shake my head in disbelief. "We were so careless in doing that. Now she knows, and she threatened to kill herself over it."

Milly gasps out loud. I can see the guilt written all over her face. She moves to touch my cheek. "Is that a hand mark?"

I pull away before she can touch me.

With wide eyes, she asks, "Did she hit you?"

"Yep, she did," I answer bluntly. I still can't believe it. Did I deserve a slap? I don't think so, but another part of me still questions it, like maybe I did. Maybe I was giving her the wrong impression, and I should have ended it when I thought she was getting too serious and overprotective of me. But I didn't, and here I am . . . at the hospital.

Milly lets out a deep sigh. "Does anyone else know about us?" she asks quietly.

I cringe. "No, she didn't tell anyone. Well, not that I'm aware of, and no one mentioned it."

Milly looks deep in thought.

I run a hand through my hair and peer off into the distance. "What will happen with Mercedez now?"

"The psychiatrist will talk to her, but if she's a danger to herself, she may be put on a psych hold."

My head falls into my hands. I'm overwhelmed. "Everything happened so fast. I knew she liked me, but I never thought she was capable of this. If I had thought she would go to these lengths, I would have ended our fling a long time ago." I feel a hand on my shoulder.

"You can't predict how someone will act. It's not your fault."

I let out a cold chuckle and glance up at her. "Then whose fault is it?"

Milly presses her lips together and stays silent.

"Whatever this is between me and you . . . it needs to be on hold for now. With everything that's going on." I throw my hands up and gesture around the hospital. I can't have a death on my conscience, no matter how much it hurts for us to have a break. Though there's a part of me that questions whether we'll ever be able to have a good time again like we did yesterday.

Tears glisten in her eyes, and I feel as though I've been stabbed in the heart. "I'm sorry," I whisper, with an aching pain in my voice. "It's not the right time." To be honest, I don't know if there'll ever be the right time for us.

She forces a smile, but the tears fall. "I understand."

I know she does, but it doesn't make this any easier.

"I've got to get back to work," Milly says, before walking away and back into the ER.

I watch her disappear through the ER doors, her shoulders stiff, her head held high. But I know her well enough to see the cracks beneath the surface. She's hurting, and I'm the one who put that pain there. My chest feels hollow, like someone's ripped out a piece of me and left nothing but an aching void.

I lean my head back against the hospital wall. The weight of everything presses down on me—Mercedez, Milly, the club, Reaper. It's all too much. I feel like I'm standing on the edge of a cliff and one wrong move will send me plummeting into the abyss.

The automatic doors slide open and a nurse steps out, her eyes scanning the area. "Reece?" she calls.

I nod. "Yeah?"

"Mercedez is stable for now," the nurse says, her tone professional but kind. "The psychiatrist is with her, and they'll likely keep her on a seventy-two-hour hold for observation."

I let out a breath. "Thanks for letting me know."

The nurse gives me a small smile before heading back inside, leaving me alone with my thoughts. I should feel relieved that Mercedez is safe, but all I feel is guilt. Guilt for not seeing the signs sooner. Guilt for letting things get this far. Guilt for dragging Milly into this mess. I settle back in my chair. There's nothing I can do, but I promised I'd be here for Mercedez. So, for now, this is where I'm staying.

TEN
REPERCUSSIONS

Milly

I WALK BACK INTO THE ER WITH MY HEART HEAVY AND MY MIND racing. I try to focus on my work, but my thoughts keep drifting back to Twitch. The way his voice cracked when he said, "It's not the right time." The way his eyes looked so broken, like he was carrying the weight of the world on his shoulders.

I know he's trying to protect me. I've spent so much of my life putting up walls, keeping people at arm's length. And just when I thought I'd found someone who could break through those walls, he's pulling away.

The psychiatrist assessed Mercedez, the doctor is keeping her on a seventy-two-hour hold. Edward said she was medicated to help her calm down. My stomach rolls at what's happened and the situation Twitch and I put ourselves in. The thought of Mercedez being willing to kill herself over us kissing pains me.

From the glares and her being so full-on with him, I knew

she liked him, but I didn't realize she was so unstable. I can't imagine it being a pleasant feeling seeing someone you like kissing someone else, but what she was willing to do over it is extreme, and I'm still not feeling okay. She and I aren't friends, but I'd never wish that on anyone.

I'm swamped. The time passes in a blur of patients, paperwork, and endless cups of coffee. By the end of my shift, I'm exhausted, both physically and emotionally.

I grab my bag and make my way to the ER waiting room where Twitch is. He hasn't moved. He must sense me because he looks up. When I see his tortured expression, I swallow hard. I hate seeing him so stressed out.

I make my way over to him. "She's on a seventy-two-hour hold. She won't have access to her phone, so she won't be able to see or speak to you. You might as well come home to the clubhouse with me."

His mouth twists, and he hesitates, so I add. "She won't know you're here. I'll keep in contact with the doctors, and they'll notify you as soon as she's ready to go back home." Home . . . I flinch. I guess I won't be staying at the clubhouse anymore upon her return.

His shoulders fall, and he blows out a breath before he stands. We walk to the car, and I struggle to find the right words. Nothing I say will comfort him. I know he won't believe it's not his fault. The silence between us is deafening as we hit the dirt road leading to the clubhouse.

"I'm really sorry this happened," I say softly.

He shakes his head. "Oh, no. This is all on *me*."

"No—" I start, but he cuts me off.

"Milly," he says seriously, his voice firm. "I mean it. Don't even think about blaming yourself. This is *all* me. *I* should have seen the signs. *I* should have stopped this thing between me and her a long time ago, but I didn't. So that's on me . . . only me."

"No, Twitch," I reply curtly, my tone sharper than intended. "Nothing's on you. *She* pulled out a knife. You could have gotten hurt. You're not responsible for *her* actions."

He lets out a heavy sigh, and I can see the guilt weighing on him. His pain sinks into me.

We pull up outside the clubhouse and head inside in silence. The moment we step through the door, everyone in the living area crowds around us.

"How's she doing?" asks Dolly, worry coating her tone.

I glance at Twitch, giving him the space to answer.

"She's on a seventy-two-hour psych hold," he says, his voice strained. "They're concerned she might hurt herself again. She was very upset." He cringes, and I know he's thinking about her screaming his name. I can only imagine how traumatic all of this has been for him. He clears his throat. "So, they medicated her."

"She's in good hands," I add, trying to reassure everyone.

"I need a drink," Twitch mutters, sounding utterly exhausted. I watch him walk to the bar, where the men immediately join him, taking seats by his side.

Me and Twitch thought we could get away with it. I should have known better. When it comes to us, nothing is ever that easy. Now we're on the verge of everyone finding out about us, because when Mercedez comes back to the clubhouse, she'll want to end us. I glance at my brother. Should we be upfront and honest before Mercedez says something to him?

My heart aches at the thought of fighting with my brother. I can't lose him and Twitch because of my carelessness.

The ol' ladies make their way over to me. "How are you doing?" Ivy asks, her frown deep with concern. She doesn't need to say anything else; the look on her face says it all.

"When the ambulance door opened, I never imagined it would be her," I admit. "I was shocked."

"I wonder why it happened. Did Twitch tell you?" Sophie asks, her curiosity as sharp as ever.

"I'm not too sure." I hate lying, but I don't have much of a choice right now.

"I heard her yelling at someone," Elena says, her voice thoughtful.

I suck in a breath, my chest tightening.

"But I didn't hear what it was about or who she was yelling at."

Relief washes over me.

"She was yelling at Twitch," Ava says. "When I put Hope down, I heard him yelling for help. When I went into his room, he was holding Mercedez, who was crying hysterically."

"He must have been with someone else," Sophie says with conviction. "There's no other explanation for her going crazy like that. How long have they been close?"

"Since before I came here," Elena answers. "I was the first ol' lady, so . . . over five years."

Twitch and I didn't think through the consequences. We were so blinded by lust and the pull to be together that we ignored everything else. And now Mercedez is in the hospital because of it. I lose control when I'm with him. My entire world becomes about him. I was so foolish to think we could escape the restraints of our friendship. Instead, we've only created more drama.

"Do you think she'll come back here after her stay at the hospital?" Ava asks.

"I don't think she has family. I've never known her to even talk about her family," Elena says. "So I don't know where else she'd go."

"Twitch probably wouldn't let her go anywhere else,"

Sophie says, shaking her head. "The look of horror on his face . . . He probably wants to keep a close eye on her. And I'm sure the club wants to know she's safe too. They take care of the sweet butts. If he was with someone else, that's clearly over now. She's made sure of that."

My heart breaks at her comment.

Viper makes his way over to me. "Do you have a moment? I burned my leg on the exhaust of my motorcycle today. Can you take a look?"

Sophie snorts. "Well, maybe you shouldn't have been doing burnouts with Axle," she says with a pout.

I crouch down and lift his jean leg. The burn is red, mottled, and wet looking. It must be painful. "It's a second-degree burn. Did you put any cold water on it when it happened?"

He nods. "Yeah, but it's still tender."

"Yes, it will be for a while. Let me grab the first aid kit out of the kitchen. I'll be back." I head to the kitchen, grab the kit, and return with sterile nonstick dressing, antibiotic ointment, and gloves. Kneeling beside him, I apply the cream and dressing. "Don't break any blisters that form. Change this dressing twice a day. If you notice any signs of infection, you'll need to see a doctor for antibiotics."

"Thanks, doc," he says with a cheerful grin.

"That's okay. It's been a big day. I think I'll hit the shower and go to bed." I say good night to everyone and drag myself upstairs to my room. My feet feel heavy, and so does my heart. I can't believe everything that's happened today.

The shower washes away the tears for what Twitch and I could have been. With Mercedez living in the clubhouse, we'll never have the chance to even spend time together again. Just being with him is fun, and I value the friendship we've made.

I feel like I've never had it easy; I've had to fight my way through everything. Like not having a family with our real mom and dad. Then, despite my struggles at school and even though I am relatively smart, I had to work my ass if to get through my exams because I still had to work hard to get where I am. Now, God forbid I like someone, but because of who he is and with everything that's happened, there's sure to be no future in it.

During the days that follow, Twitch barely speaks to me apart from asking about Mercedez. There's nothing to report back on; she's with the psychiatrists and their team. He's been at the bar drinking a lot, even while I've been at work during the day. I get it, I do. The guilt is eating him alive, but there's no convincing him it wasn't his fault. Every time I see him at the bar, my stomach twists. I hate the thought of him spiraling into depression again because of Mercedez.

The doctor called Twitch earlier today, and he informed everyone that he's picking her up this evening. She's been cleared to come home to the clubhouse. As soon as I hear the news, I go upstairs and start packing my bag. I can't stay here. Not with her coming back.

There's a knock on the door, and when I turn, Twitch is standing in the doorway. His face is a mix of exhaustion and sadness.

I give him a small, sad smile. "Don't worry, I won't be here when she gets back."

He takes a step toward me but stops, his hands clenching at his sides. "But I don't want you to go."

I blink back the tears threatening to spill. It's hard for him too—I can see that. "I have to. I don't want to upset her again, and . . ."—I lower my voice—"I can't risk her telling my brother. She's unstable, and frankly, she needs to heal. I don't want to stress her out." But deep down, there's a part of me that hates giving in to her. I frown at the thought. It's not fair, but I know leaving is the right thing to do. Still, it feels like

I'm losing my home. This place has become my sanctuary, and I don't want to leave.

"I know," he whispers sadly, his voice heavy with regret. "I'm sorry it's come to this." He looks so defeated.

I have an urge to hug him tightly, but I don't. Self-control is something I need to learn with him. I blink away the tears and force myself to keep packing. "I'm sorry too. I'm almost finished. I'll be out of here. Hopefully, she'll get better soon." I pause, my voice softening. "Just be careful and don't lead her on again."

He flinches, and I hate myself for saying it, but it needs to be said. "It's not fair for you to pretend to be with her just to make her happy. You shouldn't have to give up your happiness for her."

His voice breaks as he replies, "I can't be the reason she hurts herself."

I want to tell him that he can't live his life miserable because of her manipulation, but I keep it to myself. Instead, I turn back to my suitcase and zip it closed. When I look up again, he's gone.

I drag my suitcase downstairs, my heart heavy with every step. The clubhouse sounds quieter than usual, but a few people are still around. Bomber, Viper, Reaper, and Twitch are sitting at the bar. My brother spots me first, his eyebrows shooting up as he strides over.

"Where are you going?" Reaper asks, his tone curt.

I force a smile. "Home."

"But why?" he asks, frowning. "This is your home too. You know that, right?"

I wrap my arms around him, pulling him into a tight hug. "I know," I whisper. I try to keep my emotions in check as I step back. "Thank you for having me, but you know what I'm like." I smirk, trying to lighten the mood. "I'm an introvert. I like my quiet home."

It's a lie. I've loved staying here, surrounded by family. This place feels more like home than anywhere else ever has. But I can't tell him that. Not now.

He sighs, his shoulders slumping. "Okay, but you're welcome back whenever you want. That room is yours."

Warmth spreads through me. We haven't been as close as we were before he left for war, but moments like this remind me that he still cares. "Thanks," I say, my voice soft. "I'm sure I'll see you soon anyway."

I glance at the men at the bar. "See you guys later."

"Bye," they reply in unison.

"Sad to see you go," Viper adds with a grin.

"Me too," I admit quietly. "Night, everyone."

I walk out of the clubhouse, suitcase in hand. The moment I slide into the driver's seat of my car, the tears I've been holding back finally fall. I grip the steering wheel tightly, my chest aching with the weight of everything I'm leaving behind.

Twitch

I watch her leave from the bar, my drink untouched in front of me. The sound of her car starting and pulling away feels like a punch to the gut. I want to run after her, to tell her to stay, but I can't. Not with Mercedez coming back. Not with everything that's happened.

Reaper's voice pulls me out of my thoughts. "Are you okay?"

I glance at him, forcing a nod. "Yeah."

He doesn't look convinced, but he doesn't push. Instead,

he takes a sip of his whiskey and turns back to the conversation with Bomber and Viper. I stare at my drink, the amber liquid catching the light, but I can't bring myself to take a sip. My stomach churns at the thought of Milly leaving, at the thought of Mercedez coming back.

I don't know how to fix this. I don't even know if it can be fixed. All I know is that I've made a mess of everything, and now I'm stuck trying to pick up the pieces.

The hours pass in a blur, and before I know it, I hear a car pulling up outside, signaling Mercedez's return. I stand, my legs feeling like lead as I make my way to the door. The sweet butts picked her up because I was drinking today. When Mercedez gets out of the car, she looks fragile, her face pale, but once she sees me, her face brightens.

"Twitch," she says softly.

"I'm here," I reply, stepping forward to help her inside. She leans on me, her grip tight, and I can feel the weight of her dependence on me. It's suffocating, but I don't let it show.

As we step into the clubhouse, all eyes are on us. The room is silent, the tension thick enough to cut with a knife. I guide her to the couch, where she sits down, her hands trembling in her lap.

Reaper clears his throat, breaking the silence. "Mercedez, it's good to have you back. If you need anything, let us know."

She nods, her eyes darting to me. "I just need Twitch."

I force a smile, but inside I feel like I'm drowning.

ELEVEN

MERCEDEZ'S ULTIMATUM

Twitch

I HEAR AXLE'S LAUGH BEFORE I SEE HIM. WHEN I TURN, HE walks into the computer room with a cheeky smirk. "I see you're still hiding out in here."

I frown, unable to hide how I'm feeling. Usually I'd laugh at Axle's digs, but not today. Not after Mercedez has been home for two days. I've been struggling hardcore.

Axle's smile slips. "What's up?" His tone switches to concern.

I shrug, torn. My stomach stirs again—it's been upset for days. "I don't know what to do or how to act with Mercedez being home. I'm walking on eggshells around her, scared that any wrong move could make her want to kill herself again. She refuses to go to counseling. I checked her meds—she's not taking them either."

Axle's eyes widen.

"Sorry, I didn't mean to unload on you." He's not the deep and meaningful type, but I need . . . *someone* to talk to.

He steps toward me and leans on the computer desk. "Don't apologize. I didn't realize it was that bad and she's not trying to get better. She seems like her normal self."

"Yeah . . ." I let out a deep sigh. Because I haven't tried to push her away or set boundaries yet. I'm scared she'll do something drastic . . . like go to Reaper.

"I heard the gossip, but why did she lose her shit anyway?" he asks curiously.

I avert my gaze, considering my words carefully, but I'm desperate to talk to him about it. "I met someone else."

Axle inches back. "Wow, man, that's awesome."

My lips curve slightly as I think of Milly. "She's incredible. Like no one I've ever met, but Mercedez found out and said if I chose another woman, she'd kill herself."

Axle scoffs. "That's bullshit, man. I've lost a lot of respect for the sweet butts over the years with all the drama, and I feel bad for Mercedez, I do, but don't let her ruin your life. If you don't want to be with her, don't be with her. She'll get over it, and if not, she can go back to the hospital. You're *not* responsible for her. She's a big girl and can take care of herself."

I blink, surprised by Axle's words.

He tilts his head, looking puzzled. "What?"

"I guess I didn't expect that to come from your mouth."

He chuckles and reaches over to rough up my hair. "I joke around all the time, but I'm still your club brother, and I give a shit. I've dealt with the sweet butt crap, and they aren't worth it—no matter what they're threatening. What about this mystery woman? What's going on with her now?"

My throat tightens. "I had to put it on hold."

"Don't be an idiot," he warns. "You'll regret losing the one that matters. I can't even imagine my life without Elena." He has a point.

"I don't want to lose her. I just want to get Mercedez better in the meantime." My hand goes to my chest. "There's this overwhelming weight of guilt and worry. I still care about what happens to Mercedez. For years, I've been close with her. I don't know if I'd recover if she killed herself because of me."

Axle puts a hand on my shoulder and squeezes. "She's not your responsibility, and I think you should tell the rest of the club what you're going through. At least Reaper and Bomber should know about Mercedez. If she's not going to counseling or taking her meds, it's only a matter of time before she loses it again. And if she hurts herself, the cops might come asking questions."

The thought of even talking to Reaper about this makes me cringe. "I guess you're right. Reaper and Bomber should be informed." My shoulders are tense, and I frown. "I'm frustrated that I can't manage this myself. But I can't force Mercedez to do anything. The only control I have is over *my* actions."

"You two might be friends, but you owe her nothing. You're a good guy, but Mercedez knows this, and she's using it against you. Don't fall into the trap. If you are falling for this other chick, don't let her go because of this. You think you'll regret hurting Mercedez—you'll regret losing this other chick even more. Trust me."

Deep down, I know he's right, but I'm unsure of how to navigate my way through everything. "Thanks for the chat."

Axle winks. "I'm smart. You should listen to me."

I chuckle. "You do have brains after all."

"Oh, fuck off," he says, laughing.

When Axle leaves, I decide I need more chocolate. I pat my stomach. I'm turning into a slob. I put it down to stress.

When I enter the kitchen, Ivy, Ava, and Elena are having coffee. I smile at them.

"Have you spoken to Milly?" Ivy asks me with a raised eyebrow.

I've been meaning to, but I'm at a loss for words. Milly doesn't deserve any of this. "No, have you?"

"She's been busy at work, taking extra shifts, so I haven't had much of a chance to really talk to her."

I don't miss the small bite in her tone.

"Something's wrong with her," Ava says. "She's real quiet with me, and she's never been like that. I'm getting worried."

I stiffen.

Ivy gives me a pointed look, like she knows *exactly* why and is blaming me.

"Maybe she's just busy with work. Her job is stressful, and those twelve-hour shifts must be exhausting," Elena adds.

Ava shakes her head. "No, there's something else. She's usually open with me about everything, but whatever it is, she won't confide in me. I have no idea what it is. I wish she had never left the clubhouse." Her voice is somber.

"Maybe she thought she wasn't part of the club family, so she left to give us space to deal with the Mercedez incident," Ivy suggests.

I press my lips together and narrow my eyes at Ivy. She's getting a bit too close to the real reason for Milly leaving, and I don't like it.

"It could be. Maybe I'm reading too much into it," Ava says with a frown. "I just miss her presence here. She *is* part of the club family. I'll have to remind her of that."

"I agree," Ivy replies. "Perhaps it's because she doesn't have an ol' lady jacket like the rest of us." She looks directly at me as she says it, her tone pointed.

What the fuck? I shake my head at Ivy, trying to keep my expression neutral.

"Milly doesn't need one though," says Elena. "She's already part of the family."

"I agree," Ivy says again, her gaze still locked on me. "She shouldn't have to avoid spending time with her family and friends because of sweet butt drama."

"Do you think she'll come back and stay here again with us?" Ava asks, her voice filled with hope. It makes me feel like an even bigger piece of shit.

"I'm not too sure," Ivy replies. "Maybe we should have a barbecue soon and organize it for when Milly is free."

"Great idea. I'll talk to Reaper," Ava says cheerfully.

My heart races. How is Mercedez going to react to seeing Milly? Will she lose it again? Will she tell Reaper? I remove myself from the conversation, heading into the pantry. I pull out my chocolate stash from behind the massive bag of rice, unwrap it, and snap off half the block. My mouth waters as I take a massive bite, shoving the rest into my jacket pocket. I make my way out, ignoring Ivy's stare.

Mercedez rushes toward me from the lounge. "There you are!" she says with a lively smile, slipping her hand into mine.

I pull my hand away lightly, trying not to make a scene. "I'm updating the computer software right now. It's going to take a while."

"Aww, when can we spend some time together?" Her face is full of optimism, but it only makes my stomach churn.

"I . . . umm . . . I'm not sure," I stammer, my pulse skyrocketing.

She pouts.

"Have you taken your medication today?" I ask, already knowing the answer because I checked this morning.

"Of course I have," she says cheerily.

Such a liar. She hasn't touched her meds. But I don't want to start an argument or make her think I'm spying on her. "That's good." I take a step back. "Well, I'd better get this computer update done." I tilt my head toward the computer room.

"Oh, okay. Well, hopefully, you don't take too long."

I clip my head in a nod and stride toward the computer room. I'll get some work done, then I'll have to talk to Reaper and Bomber. Dread assaults my body. It's early, but I could down a few beers already.

I eat the rest of the chocolate while updating the system. It doesn't take long to finish, but I need the time to gather my thoughts before approaching Reaper. When I'm done, I stand, crack my neck to the sides, and go in search of him.

Mercedez runs out from the lounge again, but I put my hand up to stop her. "I need to talk to Reaper privately. It's club business."

She knows she isn't privy to that information. Her shoulders fall, and she nods before retreating back into the lounge.

I search the house, then go outside, where I find Reaper and Bomber sitting at the table, watching the kids play on the swing set with Ava and Hope. I stride toward them and take a seat beside Bomber. "Have you guys got a minute to talk? It's important."

Reaper's brows furrow and Bomber turns, giving me his full attention.

"We've always got time for you, Twitch," Reaper says.

He's too good to me. If he knew what I've done, he wouldn't be saying that. I take a deep breath. "I'm concerned about Mercedez. She refuses to go to counseling and isn't taking her meds. I don't want a repeat of last time, so I wanted you two to be aware of what's going on."

There's a heavy silence.

"Thanks for keeping me up to date with it," Reaper says finally. "I never asked, but what pushed her over the edge?"

I look down at my feet, struggling to keep my breathing even. "I met someone," I say quietly, then look at them. "It didn't go down well. She said she would kill herself if I chose the other woman."

Reaper's jaw tightens. "I want her to get better, but I'm not putting up with jealous bullshit in my clubhouse," he says firmly. "Would you like me to ask her to leave?"

I swallow hard, stunned. "You'd ask her to leave for me?"

"Of course I would," says Reaper. "You're a club member. She's been here for a long time, but you're family—you're my brother."

I flinch. I don't know if I deserve that title right now.

"And you will always be a priority over the sweet butts," Reaper finishes, while my guilt pushes my stomach into my throat.

I really am an asshole to such a good guy, who's always been there for me. I take a moment to consider my options, but I'm still stuck in the same position. I want Mercedez to get better, and I think she'll get better quicker if I'm around. I'd like to think she could get over me eventually. She's been here for a long time, and I don't know if she has any friends or family outside the club. I don't have it in me to callously drop her off and wish her good luck just to make my life easier, but I'm exhausted already and it's been only two days. I'm drained, like she's sucking the life out of me.

"I'll manage it from my end, and if she gets worse, I'll keep you guys updated."

"Are you sure?" asks Bomber, his tone skeptical. "That's a lot of pressure to put on yourself."

"I want her to get better first, then I can see how she's doing and how to proceed."

Bomber shakes his head and glances at Reaper. "That's a bad idea. She's a liability. We don't need cops around if she goes through with it." Bomber's always blunt and straight to the point.

Bomber peers at me, his expression hard. "Are you planning on staying single for the rest of your life or being in a relationship with her? Because those will be your only options. She's manipulated you once to get what she wants. She won't hesitate to do it again."

Reaper glances between us. "I trust Twitch knows what he's doing. You'll have to keep us updated on her progress."

He trusts me . . . Well, he shouldn't.

"I'll be in the computer room if you need me."

I walk away but I hear Bomber mutter, "This is going to end badly."

I briefly close my eyes. I hope not. As I open the back door, Reaper calls out my name, so I turn.

"Are you all right?" he asks, worry lining his tone.

I try to muster up a smile, but I'm not sure if it comes across as a grimace. "Yeah," I reply in a cheerful voice, even though I feel anything but.

"We're here for you," he adds.

"Thanks," I mutter, though I don't deserve his kindness.

I stay in the computer room as long as I can, losing myself in games until the bustle of voices downstairs pulls me back to reality. The smell of roasted chicken wafts through the air, and my stomach growls faintly. Usually I'm a pig when it comes to food, but lately . . . apart from chocolate, I haven't been able to stomach much at all.

There's a knock at the door, and I turn to see Mercedez standing there. "Dinner's nearly ready," she says, her voice light.

"Thanks, but I think I might go to bed early. I'm not feeling so great."

She frowns and goes to take a step toward me, but I shake my head firmly. A silent reminder: She's not allowed in here.

"Can I come into your room later then? I don't care if you're sick," she says, her tone shifting to something softer, almost coaxing.

My jaw clenches. "No, I told you. I like to sleep by myself."

"I can make you feel better," she coos, her voice dripping with seduction.

I'm trying my best not to be an asshole, but there's only so many times I can say the word *no*. "No, I don't need that from you," I reply, my tone sharper than I intended. The truth is, I don't want *anything* from her.

Her lips press together into a thin line. She looks around before speaking again. "You know . . . I heard Ava on the phone earlier."

I don't say anything and wait for her to keep going because I have no idea what she's going on about.

"She was on the phone with Milly, asking her to come to a barbecue." The way she spits out Milly's name, with utter disgust, makes my blood boil. Milly has been nothing but good to her. "Was that your idea?" she snaps.

"No," I answer defensively, my voice firm. "The women are close to Milly. They miss her. She's an important part of people's lives here." I don't know what Mercedez expects from me. Just because she's jealous doesn't mean Milly is going to stop having friends and family. For Mercedez to think the world revolves around her is pathetic.

Her eyes narrow into a death stare, and I notice her fists clench at her sides. For a moment, I wonder—if I were standing closer, would she have slapped me again?

"You need to decide what's more important to you," she hisses, her voice low and venomous. "The club or Milly. Because if you don't make me your ol' lady, I'm going to tell Reaper everything."

My world stops. Her words slam into me and my hands start to shake. "Get out!"

She yelps and dashes out, and I slam the door behind her, the sound reverberating through the walls. *Fuck her!* Every time I talk to her, I get whiplash. She goes from pretending everything is back to normal to threatening me. She realized she wasn't getting her own way, so she had to resort to saying whatever it takes for her to be an ol' lady.

I pace the room. How the hell do I choose between my brothers and Milly? I hate Mercedez for putting me in this position, but I'm just as angry at myself. I let my fling with her go on for too long, and now it's come back to haunt me.

But what if I choose Milly and she doesn't choose me? Or worse—what if I'm the reason Milly loses her relationship with her only close blood relative? Reaper is her family, and I can't be the one to take that away from her.

I shouldn't be the reason Milly loses her loved ones. I know she likes me, but I like her more. It physically hurts my chest that she's not mine. I say I like her, but Mercedez has traumatized me. The way she's acted—the jealousy, the manipulation—has left a bad taste in my mouth. As much as I hate to admit it, it's made me scared to jump into any kind of relationship with the opposite sex.

And Milly? She deserves better. She deserves someone stable, someone who can give her the life she deserves. Someone like that other doctor. Reaper would approve of him too.

I hate that Milly and I are the casualties in all of this. My heart is tortured at the thought of her moving on, but maybe it's for the best. Even though being with Mercedez will make me miserable—because I can't deal with her malice and manipulation—if it means Milly will be happy, if it means she'll keep her family and find a man who truly deserves her, then it's the least I can do. Even if it's to my own demise.

TWELVE
THE BARBECUE

Milly

LAST NIGHT AT WORK WAS SURPRISING. DURING MY BREAK, Edward asked me to lunch again. I went because he's a friendly guy and is turning out to be a good friend. We chatted, and I couldn't resist teasing him about how the nurses and patients practically have love hearts coming out of their eyes when they see him. It's become my favorite form of entertainment—watching the young nurses turn beet red when they talk to him is hilarious.

But then, out of nowhere, he asked me if I wanted to go on a date. I froze. My heart started pounding and my breathing became erratic. I was in total shock. I stumbled over my words, stuttering like an idiot. My throat was dry, and I finally managed to say, "I'll get back to you with an answer soon." It's been on my mind ever since. I'm torn because he's a great guy, but I can't deny my feelings for Twitch.

I push the thoughts to the back of my mind as I cautiously walk into the clubhouse. My heart is thumping in my chest until I see two of my close friends, Ava and Ivy. They rush toward me, and Ivy squeals as they hug me. I'm sandwiched between them.

"I've missed you," Ivy says, and my chest warms. It's nice to be missed and cared for.

Ava inches back. "Me too. I know it hasn't been long, but it feels like ages since I've spoken to you. Is everything okay?"

No, it's not, but I smile. "Yes, sure. Sorry I've been quiet. I've been so busy with work." I swallow down the lump in my throat. The lies keep piling up, and I hate it. I'm not a person who deceives others, especially my friends, but I feel as though I'm backed into a corner with no way out.

Ivy's face softens. At least she knows what I'm going through. I need one friend to talk to. The whole situation is driving me crazy.

"Do you need any help in the kitchen?" I ask Ava, desperate to change the subject.

"Oh, no, it's all sorted. The sweet butts are helping."

I cringe at the thought of Mercedez. Today is going to be interesting . . .

"I'd better go back and make sure everything is ready. The men are outside by the barbecue. Go grab a drink and relax."

I smile at Ava. She's so lovely, and I'm grateful my brother met someone as sweet as her. She's tried to make this clubhouse feel like home.

Once Ava leaves, Ivy turns to me, her expression serious. "Okay . . . what's really going on?"

I glance about, seeing no one close by. It seems everyone is out in the backyard. "Mercedez told Twitch she'd kill herself if he decided to be with me, so I left the clubhouse. I didn't want to cause any more trouble, and even though I hate what Mercedez has caused, I don't want to make the situation worse. I can see she's in pain, but . . ." My voice trails off as dark emotions settle over me like a shadow, a heaviness I can't seem to shake.

Ivy places a comforting hand on my arm, silently encouraging me to continue.

"It's been so hard at home." I take a deep breath, trying to calm the flood of emotions rushing to the surface. "I didn't realize how much I missed being here. Twitch was there when I had nightmares, and I got to see friendly faces all the time. My house is too quiet. I'm not big on socializing, but it feels right here." I glance around the clubhouse. "At home, I'm lonely." The admission sends a ripple through my body.

I've never been someone with a lot of friends. I've always tried to be kind, but I didn't forge real friendships until I met the women at the clubhouse. And now, with my new friends, I don't feel welcome here because of Mercedez. Any mistake could be catastrophic for me and Twitch.

Ivy gives me another tight hug. "Mercedez seems like nothing happened, to be honest."

Goosebumps erupt on my arms. "What do you mean?" My breath seizes. "Are Twitch and her back to what they used to be like?"

She shakes her head. "Not back to that. He still doesn't allow her into his room. He spends most of his time in the office or in his bedroom. I overhead Axle say he's hiding from Mercedez in there. I've been watching Twitch. He flinches when she gets too close or puts a hand on his arm, but he's not exactly telling her off for it. I think he's trying to keep the peace. He's in a terrible position."

My gut drops. I rub my aching chest, trying to ease the pain. "It's not fair." He's trying to do the right thing, but it doesn't make it hurt any less.

Ivy links her arm in mine. "Try to ignore it. We've missed you, and I want you to have a good day. You're always welcome here, and, hopefully, Mercedez will grow up and come to her senses."

I give Ivy a small smile. I very much doubt it.

We walk through the clubhouse and out the back door. The smell of barbecuing meat greets my nostrils. The beat of heavy metal thumps in the background. A few of the men's heads turn our way, and a smile spreads across my brother's face. He strides over and pulls me into a bear hug. "It's good to see you back," he says warmly.

I chuckle. It hasn't been long at all, but it's nice to see everyone again.

All the ol' ladies are gathered around the large wooden table, so I take a seat next to Zara and Ivy. Twitch and Rage are also there. I give everyone a tight smile, but I refuse to look at Twitch for too long, afraid of what I might see—or feel. Zara smiles, though she looks a little pale.

"It's good to see you again," I say. "How's the pregnancy going?"

Her smile falls. "I'm still really sick and lethargic all the time, but I think it's part of being pregnant."

"Did the doctor give you any nausea tablets?"

She nods. "They work if I can keep them down and not throw up that day."

She's responsible, but I reply with, "Just don't miss any of your prenatal appointments."

"I won't." She bites her bottom lip, hesitating. "I'm scared something will go wrong."

I put my hand on hers. "That's normal. If you ever have any questions, let me know. I'm always here for you."

Her shoulders relax, and she gives me a small, grateful smile. "Thanks so much."

Ava, along with the sweet butts, bring out the side dishes —corn on the cob, fried rice, mac and cheese, and salad—and centers them on the table. I see Mercedez, but I avoid making eye contact. I just need to get through today. Ava wouldn't take no for an answer when she invited me, and when I said I couldn't make it, she made sure the barbecue didn't happen until I was available. I couldn't say no to that. If I had, she would've become even more suspicious about why I've been keeping my distance.

"Lunch is ready," Reaper declares, and the men take a seat around the wooden table next to their partners.

The meat is put in the middle, and we all fill our plates.

"So . . . Milly, how's McDaddy doing?" Sophie purrs his name in a teasing, seductive tone.

I choke on my saliva, and everyone glances my way as Ivy pats my back. I see Mercedez place her hand on Twitch's arm. My stomach twists, and my nostrils flare as I glare at her hand. He doesn't ask her to move it. My fists clench under the table. If they're close again, I guess I can freely date too.

"He ummm . . . asked me out on a date," I say, and then take a long swig from my wine to avoid looking at anyone.

"What?" Twitch asks, his voice rougher than usual. His eyes widen as he realizes his outburst.

McDaddy asking me out was unexpected and random. He enjoys spending time with me, but I'm torn about what to do. I hadn't decided until I saw Mercedez's hand on Twitch's arm. I'm not ready to get involved with someone else, but I'm overrun and burning with jealousy. The bitterness is rotting me from the inside out.

"Woohoo!" Sophie cheers. "I need a picture of this guy ASAP."

Viper raises a brow. "Really? Do you now?" he asks her.

Sophie replies, "Yes, really. I'm nosy. I'm with you now, so I need to live through all the single women."

I've been single for most of my life. I never dated much. I'm quiet and focused on my career. Working long shifts all the time and doing overtime did little for my social life. Now

I'm interested in Twitch, and I have a colleague who wants to go out on a date. Trust this to happen to me all at once.

Viper shakes his head with a smirk on his lips.

"When's the date?" Ava asks, leaning forward, clearly invested in my story.

Twitch's eyes are burning holes into my head, but I ignore him. "He suggested tomorrow night at the seafood restaurant by the beach."

Out of the corner of my eye, I see Mercedez's beaming smile. "I'm so happy for you," she says, her voice sickly sweet and dripping with fake enthusiasm.

Ivy claps. "I'm happy for you finally getting out and dating again."

"*Again*?" Reaper asks, his sharp eyes narrowing. He doesn't miss much . . . apart from me and Twitch.

My breathing quickens. "She just meant because it's been so long since I have," I reply to my brother at lightning speed, trying to cover my tracks.

"What did this doctor's background check say?" Reaper asks, glancing at Twitch.

Twitch's jaw tightens, and I can see the muscle ticking as he grinds his teeth.

I clasp and unclasp my hands, trying to stay calm.

"Twitch?" Reaper prompts again.

Twitch's eyes fly to Reaper. "Divorced. No kids. Worked his whole life. Not even a parking ticket. Pretty boring if you ask me."

I narrow my eyes at him. Well, no one asked for his opinion.

"I like boring," Reaper adds approvingly.

Of course he does. No risks.

"Have you got pepper spray just in case?" Reaper asks.

I groan at Reaper. "You taught me self-defense. I can handle myself."

Reaper's brows curve in. "That wasn't an answer to my question."

"Yes," I reply, feeling like a scolded child. "I have it."

Reaper nods his head sharply in approval. "Good to hear."

It's sweet that he's still overprotective, but I'm an adult, and it seems he forgets that sometimes.

I sit back and listen to the conversations around me. I sigh, hating that I'll miss this from now on. I miss the jokes from Axle and Viper, the banter between them and the rest of the club. I've missed seeing Hope and spending time with Ava and Ivy. This whole situation sucks. I decide to have only one glass of wine so I can leave early. I'm sure dating the doctor has pleased Mercedez, but she's so unpredictable.

I tell the club I'm tired, and I leave. The frowns on Ava's and Ivy's faces were hard to ignore. When I open my car door, I hear, "Hold on."

I turn to see Twitch jogging toward me. "You're leaving early."

Even though it's dark outside, I can see the dark circles under his eyes. I frown. He looks exhausted—a far cry from the happy man I'm used to seeing. I check to make sure no one followed him. "I am. I don't want to risk it with you-know-who."

He runs a hand through his wavy hair. "I've missed you," he breathes.

A thrill shoots through me at his words, but I give him a sad smile. "I've missed you too." Because I have—*so* much. Especially after that night we spent together. It was bliss.

"What have you been up to?" he asks shyly, scratching the back of his neck.

"Work, and I've been getting motorcycle lessons."

He smiles, but it fades quickly. "I could've spent more time with you and taught you. Maybe we can do it again."

I shake my head with a sigh. "With everything going on now, you couldn't have. I enjoyed riding so much I wanted to keep doing it. One day when I own my own bike, maybe we could ride together." It's false hope, but still hope, none-theless.

I glance up at him. He's frowning, like he's already given up. There's a tightness in my chest. "I need to know . . . have we truly ended what we had going on?"

He takes a step back, and his eyes sharpen. "Well, it seems so when you're going on dates with other people."

I scoff. "Well"—I throw back in the same tone he used—"seems like you and Mercedez are close again. That didn't take long at all."

"We. Aren't. Close."

"Could've fooled me."

He lets out a cold laugh. "You're going out on a date with the most boring person ever. But at least he meets your broth-er's checklist."

I suck in a breath. He did *not* just say that! "That's not fair. Edward's a nice guy."

"Yeah, nice . . ." he says like he threw up in his mouth. "Perfect for the MC president's sister."

"Jealousy really brings out a new side of you, Twitch."

He drags his hand down his face. "Only *you* do this to me! I've never been so jealous in my life as I am about you going out on a date with someone else." He clutches his chest. "It's like a serrated blade cutting my heart. I don't want Mercedez. I want you! But I can't do anything about it right now."

I struggle to breathe. My eyes blur.

We can't find common ground. We're stuck in a maze we can't escape, caught between our dream of being together and the reality we live in.

He leaves, and once I hear the front door shut, I open my

car door and jump in. I turn my car on, and I'm out of there, leaving the Mercedez and Twitch drama in my wake.

Once I get home, I send McDaddy a message:

> My answer is yes to the date. Tomorrow is still good for me ☺

> Yes! Looking forward to seeing you.

I should be excited to go out on a date with a handsome bachelor, but I feel nothing but that irritating sense of guilt. I hate it. Edward's a great guy, but I can't help it if I still like Twitch.

THIRTEEN
DATE NIGHT

Milly

I TURN THE MUSIC UP ON MY PHONE, TRYING TO DROWN OUT THE oppressive silence in my house. I put on an upbeat song, but it does nothing to lift my mood. If I hadn't spent time with Twitch, I'd probably be excited about this date. I've never experienced a gorgeous older man being interested in me, but here I am, moping around because all I can think about is the hurt in Twitch's eyes last night.

But I can't keep being second best to Mercedez every time she threatens him.

He thought I was moving on . . . . Am I trying to? Just seeing Mercedez's hand on Twitch's arm made me snap, and I was ready to fight fire with fire. But now, with only an hour until I have to leave for my date, the damn guilt is weighing me down. Am I leading Edward on just to get back at Twitch? The thought makes me feel like a terrible person. I've only been out of control since Twitch and I got closer. Normally I'm levelheaded, but he messes with my mind.

I walk to my wardrobe and sift through my clothes. Lack of motivation has me pulling out jeans, but I quickly put them back. It's a fancy restaurant, after all. I settle on a more formal top and a three-quarter black skirt, then get changed. I glance at myself in the mirror. *This could be my life.* The life Reaper wants for me. A man who can take care of me, who has a good career. A man who is respectful and wines and dines me.

It's such a stark contrast to the other side of my life—a man who wears a leather vest, is part of a motorcycle club, and doesn't have a "proper" job. Reaper never wanted me to be part of the club life. He struggled to even let me be the club doctor. I look back at my jeans. My life with Twitch would be simple if my brother and Mercedez weren't in the equation.

I put on some makeup before heading to my car. I peek in the visor mirror and force a smile. If there's one thing I'm good at, it's hiding my feelings and pretending to be happy. It's exhausting, but it wouldn't be fair to Edward if he thought he was the reason I wasn't enjoying myself. If the women at the hospital found out about this date, they'd be so jealous. And even though my feelings for Twitch are all over the place, I should be open to giving Edward a chance. Someone like him could make me happy. The truth is, I don't feel the same spark for Edward that I feel for Twitch. That passion, that electric pull to be near him, to feel his kiss, his touch—it's not there with Edward.

I drive to the restaurant and park where Edward is standing by his car. Getting out, I feel underdressed. I smile at him. He's dressed up in a dark navy blue suit that snugly fits him, showing off his broad shoulders.

He steps over to me and shuts my car door. "You're beautiful."

My face heats. "You look very handsome." I kiss his cheek. "I love the suit."

His lips curve up. "Oh, this old thing."

I look up at the restaurant. It's modern, with a wooden deck that wraps around it and big windows. I link my arm in his and we walk up to the restaurant entrance and through the glass door.

He speaks to the waiter, who ushers us outside to our table. The sun is setting, painting the sky in hues of orange and pink. The sound of the ocean waves lapping against the shore is soothing.

"It's spectacular," I say, taking in the view.

"It is," he replies. "The view is outstanding, and this restaurant has excellent reviews for the food."

"Would you like anything to drink?" the waiter asks.

"A glass of sauvignon blanc, please," I answer.

"And what brand, ma'am?"

"The cheapest is fine, thank you," I reply with a smile.

"The best one," Edward interjects.

"It doesn't have to be expensive," I protest. I'm easygoing, and I've learned that just because it's expensive doesn't mean it tastes any better.

"I'm paying," he offers, then looks back at the waiter. "She'll have the best that you've got."

O-kay. I let it go, and he orders a whiskey on the rocks.

"How have your two days off been?" he asks.

I cringe inwardly at the memory of yesterday. "I went to the clubhouse and saw my brother and his partner. We had a barbecue. It was good to catch up." I struggle to keep my voice even because I've missed them all.

"I'd love to meet your brother at some stage. It seems like an interesting dynamic."

Edward is moving a little fast, wanting to meet my family. I scan the floor for the waiter. Where's my wine? I'm going to need it if this is where the conversation is heading. "How have your last few days been?" I ask, steering the topic away from my brother.

"I've been decorating my home because it's been a little bare. Now, I'm not the best at it." He chuckles. "Maybe it needs a woman's touch." He gives me a long, lingering look.

I gulp. "Sorry, I'm useless at that sort of thing. I've lived in my home for a long time, and it's still bare." Not that there are many photos of family or friends or vacations I can put up anywhere. My home is clinical, like a show home that no one lives in. My thoughts turn to the clubhouse. I don't mind the mess there and the kids' toys because there's a lot of love and laughter in that place that overrides anything else.

"Still," he says, "if we have a weekend off together, it would be nice to have help from a friendly face."

I smile politely. "Yes, sure." I don't mind helping friends.

The waiter arrives with my drink, and as subtly as I can, I take a few large gulps. "And if you don't mind me asking, why did you ask me out?" I flinch.

He raises an eyebrow and smiles. "I enjoy your company, and I don't know many people here . . . but I'd be lying if I said I wasn't interested."

I take another gulp, giving him a tight smile. Unsure how to respond, I look down at the menu.

"You're quiet," he observes.

I wince. "I just . . . I don't know if I'm in the right place to be dating." If I weren't interested in Twitch, this wouldn't even be a conversation. But I am, and it's not fair to the handsome man sitting across from me.

"I get that . . . but I'm in no rush."

I divert my attention back to the menu. "The seafood marinara looks nice," I comment lamely.

He grabs a menu in front of him. "Do you like all types of seafood?"

"Yes, I love all food in general."

"What about the seafood platter for two?" he asks, pointing to the menu.

I look at the $300 price tag, and my eyes bug out of my head. "That's a lot of money."

He chuckles. "I'm sure it will be worth it."

"It better be for that price," I mutter under my breath, earning another laugh from him.

"You don't spoil yourself often, do you?" he asks, his tone softening.

I take a moment to think. "No, I don't." I'm on a good salary, but growing up poor taught me to be frugal. Even now, I struggle with spending money on things I don't absolutely need. My biggest splurge was buying a secondhand convertible, and even that felt like a guilty indulgence.

"You get one life. You can't take the money with you. Spend your money on what makes you happy."

I sigh, his words hitting a little too close to home. "I've realized lately that I've been cruising through life—working but not actually living. It's kind of sad." I rub the base of my throat, feeling a lump form. "Outside of the club, I haven't developed any real close friends. I don't go on vacations. I've rarely ever gone on dates. I've put my life on hold for my career, and now that I've made it . . . ." I trail off, looking at him. "They've brought on new staff, so I can take more time off. I actually bit the bullet and started taking motorcycle lessons."

He gives me a round of applause. "Good on you. Do you like it?"

I give him a genuine smile. "I always wanted to learn but never dared to ask my brother. A guy from the club offered me the opportunity to learn and ride on his bike, and I rode it through a parking lot. I got such a high from it that I knew right then and there I was learning no matter what." It's one thing I'm proud of myself for—finally getting out there and doing something I've always wanted to try.

"You'll have to pick me up one day when you get your full license."

I cackle, and it's loud, drawing looks from other people at the tables nearby. "I can't imagine you on the back of a motorcycle, but it would be funny to see."

The waiter returns, and we grab another round of drinks. Edward orders for us, and I try my best not to think about the ridiculous price tag.

"Are they still calling me McDaddy at the hospital?" he asks, sounding amused.

"They certainly are. You can't blame them. You're the town's shiny new single man."

He hides a smile. "Do you call me that?"

Now, this can go one of two ways. "Yes, but it's stuck now. It's your name. I'm sorry. Anything else doesn't sit right."

He laughs out loud, his shoulders shaking with amusement.

Before I can join in, I notice someone approaching. My blood runs cold as Twitch grabs a chair from a nearby table and slides it between us.

I cough, trying to mask my shock. "Um . . . is everything alright?" I ask, my voice tight, wondering what the hell he is doing here.

He gives me a sly smirk. "Yes, everything's all good. How's your date going?"

The blood rushes back to my face, and my cheeks burn with embarrassment. Twitch's devilish grin only makes it worse. He's here to ruin my date. "Why are you here, Twitch? Can't we have this chat another time?" My voice grows harsher with each word.

He chuckles, completely unfazed. "All good. Just thought I'd check up on you."

I glare at him. "Well, everything is great, so you can go now."

He looks me dead in the eyes, his lit up with amusement. "Nah, I think I'll stay."

I turn to Edward, mortified. "I'm so sorry about this . . . intrusion."

Twitch looks at Edward, his grin widening. "Oh, you don't mind, do you?"

He gives me a funny look but smiles politely. He's taking this well. Most men would have gotten angry at Twitch. "As long as it's okay with Milly."

I open my mouth to object, but Twitch cuts me off. "We're best friends; she'll be fine."

"Best. Friends," I spit out, my tone dripping with sarcasm. *What is he getting at?*

Edward stands, clearly sensing the tension. "I'll go to the bar. Let the two of you talk."

My breath catches. "No, it's okay. Twitch is leaving."

Twitch grabs my drink and takes a sip, completely ignoring me. I scoff. The nerve of him!

"I'm staying," he says with a big-ass grin.

I take a few deep breaths, trying to keep calm.

"I'll be back in a bit," Edward says, walking away. I watch him leave, feeling terrible that Twitch drove him away.

"What are you doing here?" I whisper-yell, my frustration boiling over.

Twitch finishes my drink and leans back in his chair. "The real question is, what are *you* doing here? I mean, you deserve the world and all, but . . ." He looks around the restaurant, lifting his nose. "This isn't you."

I huff. "Can't I go to fancy restaurants?"

He shrugs. "You seem more chill. Like you'd be happier ordering takeout."

He's not wrong. I love being in my pajamas, eating

takeout in the comfort of my home. "What's your point?" I snap.

"Why'd you say yes to go on a date with a man you don't like to a place you don't even care about?"

I don't like the accusatory tone in his voice. "Why aren't you back at home looking after Mercedez?" I throw back in the same sharp tone he used.

He cringes. Low blow, but if the shoe fits. "I'm trying to deal with all that," he mumbles.

I immediately regret my words. "I'm sorry. I shouldn't have said that. I don't know what came over me." Being spiteful isn't who I am. "I guess I hate that we never got a chance to decide what we were going to do. She kind of decided for us . . . and still is." I rub my chest, feeling vulnerable.

He runs a hand through his hair, his expression pained. "I'm sorry. I don't know how to help her while also trying not to ruin us."

My heart beats faster. "So there is an *us*?"

His face twists with conflict, and he groans. "Don't get me wrong, I want there to be. I've never felt this way about another woman, but I don't want to be the reason you lose your brother and I lose my family."

Tears prick my eyes, and I dab at the corners to stop them from falling.

He stands abruptly. "Sorry for being an asshole. I'll go. But . . ." He hesitates, looking at the ground. "Can I stay at yours tonight?"

The hope in his voice crushes all my resolve. "I'll eat dinner and go home. I'll meet you there." I reach into my bag to grab my house keys.

He shakes his head. "I already have one."

My mouth opens to object, but he cuts me off.

"After the kidnapping," he explains. "I wanted to make

sure I could get to you if anything happened again. I've never gone inside. It's just for safety."

That shuts me up. I reluctantly nod. "Okay."

He gives me one of his cocky, seductive grins before walking away. Just the thought of seeing him again has me buzzing. He stops at the bar, exchanges a few words with Edward, and then leaves.

Edward returns to the table, and I immediately start apologizing. "I'm so sorry about that."

"It's okay," he says with a kind smile. "I could tell the two of you needed to talk. If you don't mind me asking, is he the reason you're not dating?"

I press my lips together firmly. "Frankly, I don't know what's going on myself. While I'm undecided, it's not fair to date anyone else."

He smiles, and it puts me at ease. "That's completely fine, but why aren't you with him?"

I sigh, the weight of the situation pressing down on me. "We're stuck between wanting to give a relationship a chance and hurting everyone around us. My brother warned the men that they couldn't have anything to do with me. He tolerates the friendships I've made. He's always wanted me to date someone outside the club. Twitch and I have always had a bond, even as friends. But when things changed and we got more involved, we kept it a secret. If my brother finds out, I could lose him. And Twitch . . . he could lose everything.

"My brother is big on loyalty and respect, and I don't know how I'd cope with losing my only close relative. Being in a motorcycle club, Twitch could face worse consequences for defying the president's orders, lying to him and the club, and then sleeping with his sister."

Edward leans back in his chair, his expression thoughtful as he processes everything I've just said. "Worse, as in death . . . or being kicked out of the club?" he asks cautiously.

I throw a hand up. "That's it. I don't know. Their club is tight-knit, and no one has ever defied or done anything against the club president before. I love my brother, and I can't see him killing someone over it, but I see him as my brother. I don't know him as the club president."

Edward winces, his brows furrowing "That's a lot to carry. But it seems like Twitch has risked it all for you already. If your brother is as good as a man you make him out to be, he might surprise you and be okay with it all."

I let out a bitter laugh. "My stubborn-ass brother? The one who's big on respect and loyalty? I just can't see him letting it go."

Before Edward can respond, the waiter arrives with our enormous seafood platter. Lobster, prawns, fish, oysters, and crab are arranged beautifully on the tray. It looks and smells amazing, but my appetite is gone. I force myself to take a few bites, picking at the lobster while Edward digs in. I ask him questions about his life before he moved here, but my mind is elsewhere. I'm stuck in my thoughts, eager to see Twitch again.

"Are you all right?" Edward asks, his voice pulling me back to the present.

I blink a few times, realizing I've been quiet for too long. "Yes, sorry. I'm just getting tired. I might head out if that's okay."

He smiles warmly, his understanding nature making me feel even guiltier. "Of course. It was lovely, even with the surprise visit from your friend." He chuckles. "But it was nice to get out and try a new restaurant."

I stand, and so does he. I give him a big hug, trying to show how grateful I am. "Yes, it was a good night, and we should do it again . . . as friends." My head is a big enough mess with Twitch; I don't want him to get the idea I mean something more than friends.

"Of course," he replies, his smile never faltering.

I let out a sigh of relief. He's such a good guy. "How much was it? I'll pay my half."

He shakes his head with a stern look on his face. "No, no. The man always pays."

"Thank you," I say softly. "Have a good night." I grab my bag and walk out the door, my heart heavy with conflicting emotions.

The drive home is quiet, but my hands are clammy on the steering wheel. I have no idea why I'm so nervous. My mind is a storm of thoughts, swirling with what-ifs and possibilities. Twitch mentioned the word *us*. Like it was a real possibility. The thought sends my heart racing, but optimism is quickly followed by the crushing weight of reality.

When I pull into my driveway, I notice Twitch's bike isn't there. He must have parked it farther down the street. As I step out of the car, he emerges from the shadows under the porch.

"That was quick," he says with a smirk. Always with the smartass remarks.

"What can I say . . . he's faster than you," I quip, unable to resist.

His mouth drops open in mock offense, and I can't help but laugh. The look on his face is priceless, and for a moment, the tension between us melts away.

"That wasn't funny," he says, pretending to sound hurt.

I smile. "I thought it was." I unlock the door and step inside, heading straight for my bedroom. "I need to change into my pajamas."

He leans against the doorframe. "Nothing I haven't seen before."

I stop and cross my arms, giving him a pointed look. He sighs dramatically and turns around, giving me privacy. I take a moment to gaze at him. He looks effortlessly sexy in his low-slung jeans and motorcycle cut.

I quickly change into my pajamas, the soft fabric a welcome comfort.

"How was it?"

I snort. "Well, you were there."

He chuckles. "I had to see you. I was going insane thinking you were with him." His voice is rough, which matches his declaration.

"McDaddy and I are officially *just* friends."

"Good!" He shakes his head. "Can you please not call him that?"

I smirk at the hint of jealousy in his voice. I get into bed and snuggle under the sheets. "All done," I say.

He turns around, his eyes heating as they rake over me. One thing I love about Twitch is that he looks at me like I'm wearing lingerie even when I'm in my comfiest clothes. The butterflies in my stomach are in full force as I glance at him again. I love being desired, even when I'm at my most casual.

Without hesitation, he takes off his cut and hangs it up, then strips off his jeans. My mouth waters as I remember what's underneath those boxer briefs.

"Didn't the piercing hurt?" I blurt out, immediately cringing at my lack of filter.

He smirks. "Yes, but it was only temporary."

"Are we temporary?" I ask softly, my voice tinged with sadness.

His smirk fades, and he frowns as he pulls his shirt off and tosses it to the floor. He climbs into bed beside me, and for what feels like the first time in forever, he touches me, pulling me into his arms.

"All I know is we have tonight," he murmurs, his voice low and rough. "Before the sun comes up and we have to deal with life as we know it."

I run a hand over his warm chest and then tug at his nipple ring. His body makes my restraint crumble, and I lift to place my lips against his. I've missed him. His groan of pleasure sends shockwaves through my body, and his mouth moves with mine, his tongue dancing as my heart races. Our kiss is filled with passion and unspoken wishes of what we can't have.

He grabs my hand and puts it on his cock. "This is what you do to me," he says huskily. "Every thick inch is because of you."

I grasp him and stroke him through his briefs.

He's panting but opens his eyes and starts undoing my button-up top. He grumbles when he can't undo the buttons fast enough, and I giggle. I swat him away. "I'll do it." After I take off my top, I get rid of my pants. He gets up and flips me onto my back, making me chuckle. "So impatient," I mutter.

"I'm dying over here not being inside of you."

I smile. He's dramatic, but I must admit I'm drenched. I lick my lips, entranced with the sight of his lean body. I've seen him naked a few times before, but it always feels like it's the first time.

He groans loudly. "I need to taste you first."

Before I can form a coherent word, my legs are parted and he moves down my body. He shoves his head between my legs and sucks on my clit, making me buck and gasp. "I could eat you all day," he says before his expert mouth goes back to my clit.

He plunges two fingers inside of me. I squirm, but he holds me firm, fucking me with his mouth and hand, quickly and unrelenting. He slides the metal ball of the tongue piercing over my clit, and I buck at the sensation. It is intense. My body is on fire, and I'm gasping, trying to breathe. I pull at his hair as the orgasm crashes through me without warning and my muscles clamp down on his fingers. I can't hold back —I scream his name.

My body collapses as I savor every wave of pleasure that hits me. He moves up my body until he hovers over me and says, "Taste yourself." He presses his lips to mine, so I open as he commands. My arousal is sweet on his tongue.

When he's had enough of the torture, he parts my thighs. I'm eager to have him bury himself inside me again. He thrusts forward, and even though I'm wet, his size is still overwhelming. He sucks on my neck and teases me with sweet kisses, and I relax. He pulls out and thrusts at a steady pace.

"It's been forever since I've been inside you." He places kisses on the most sensitive part of my neck. "Far too long," he murmurs, and I wholeheartedly agree.

He quickens his pace until he's fucking me like a man possessed, hitching my right leg up higher until he's in deeper, hitting my G-spot. I moan louder as I hold on for dear life. My fingers dig deeper into his back as I'm getting closer to that sweet spot, and the moment his fingers connect with my oversensitive clit I fall apart into a million pieces in his arms.

"You feel so good," he rasps. He kisses me hard as he chases his own release. His body finally bucks as he fills me. He collapses beside me, panting and wiping the sweat off his forehead.

"Lucky I'm on birth control," I murmur jokingly.

His eyes bulge. "Fuck, I'm sorry, I forgot." He looks away, confused. "I've never forgotten." His eyes pin me. "I blame you. You and your witchcraft."

I laugh out loud. "*My* witchcraft?"

He nods. "Yes, *you* have this control over me."

I smile, secretly loving it.

I go to the bathroom, and when I come back he's already

asleep. He seems more tired than usual. The Mercedez drama is taking a toll on him. I should give him a break, but it tears me apart that because of Mercedez's manipulative ways, I have to be second best. That he fell asleep quickly in my bed is a compliment—he feels at ease in my home. I snuggle into him and moments later fall asleep.

The loud sound of a phone ringing startles me awake. The ringtone isn't mine. Twitch groans, fumbling for the phone until he picks it up. I catch a glimpse of the screen before he answers, and my stomach drops. It's Mercedez.

"Hello," he answers groggily.

The room is quiet, so I hear every word.

"Where are you?" Mercedez demands, her tone sharp.

"Wait, what?" Twitch sounds confused. "I fell asleep at my mom's. Why?"

"So you're not with Milly?" she asks in a fiery voice.

"No, I'm not," he replies confidently.

"I warned you, Twitch. If you don't make me your ol' lady, I'm telling everyone."

Dread takes my chest hostage, making it hard to breathe.

Twitch stands abruptly, putting the phone on loudspeaker. He grabs his shirt and pulls it on aggressively before sitting back down. "You think threatening me is going to make me fall in love with you?" he snaps.

I'm impressed he's standing up for himself, but the tension in the room is suffocating.

"Don't make me out to be the bad guy," Mercedez hisses. "I get what I want, and you got the freedom of screwing the president's sister without him finding out. You really think your MC family is going to want you if they find out about the betrayal?"

I gasp, the weight of her words hitting me like a punch to the gut.

Twitch makes eye contact with me, his expression hard.

"I'm coming back to the clubhouse now," he says, then hangs up and rushes to grab his pants. "I'm sorry. I've got to go. I took the tracker off my bike, but she's convinced I'm here with you, and, well . . . she's not wrong."

The realization that this is all we'll ever be hits me with full force. There's a deep ache beneath my ribs, like all four chambers of my heart have been crushed.

He kisses my cheek, but I don't feel it. The moment he leaves, tears fall freely down my face.

FOURTEEN
DEATH BY A THOUSAND CUTS

Milly

Sleeping is impossible. I toss and turn for the remainder of the night, my mind replaying every moment with Twitch. Today is a workday, but I called in sick. I've had barely a few hours of sleep, and I know I won't be any good at work like this—miserable and distracted. I never take sick days, but today I just can't face it.

My phone rings, and my heart leaps. I'm hoping it's Twitch, but when I glance at the screen, I see it's Edward. I let out a long sigh, feeling foolish for letting my guard down with Twitch. I should've known better.

"Hello," I answer, trying to sound normal.

"Hey, I was told you were sick. I wanted to check you got home okay and it wasn't food poisoning or anything."

"No, the food was great," I reply, forcing a small laugh. "I just didn't get much sleep and thought I'd do more harm than good if I showed up today."

"That's not good. I hope you get some rest," he says, his

voice warm with concern. "By the way, do you remember that older man who lost his wife in the shooting?"

I pause, my chest tightening. "Ah, yes, I remember him." How could I forget? He blamed me for his wife's death. No hard feelings, though—I can't imagine how hard it must be to lose the person you love most. My eyes water as I think about Twitch. He's not just some guy. He's *the* guy, the one I want to spend the rest of my life with.

"The man came in today asking for you," Edward continues. "He still looked stressed out. I wasn't sure if he was planning to apologize for his behavior last time, but I told him you'd most likely be in tomorrow."

I frown. "The man seemed traumatized the last time I saw him. Are you sure he wanted to apologize, because there's no need, really?"

"He didn't say, but I can't imagine him needing to yell at you again."

Edward's optimism is almost endearing. Grief hits people differently, so I better prepare myself for tomorrow—whether it's an apology or another round of blame. It could go either way.

"Well, thanks for letting me know," I say.

"Hopefully, I'll see you tomorrow."

I wince. "Yes, I should be in." Who am I kidding? Of course I'll go in. I'm going to go stir-crazy today, and the guilt of putting my own feelings before work is eating at me.

We say goodbye and I put my phone down, only for it to ring again. I groan loudly, frustrated that I can't even have a moment to dwell. When I see Ivy's name on the screen, I soften. Ivy is one of my safe people.

"Hello," I answer, unable to fake cheeriness.

"Oh no," her voice drops. "Is everything okay?"

My pathetic love life makes me pause. "I've realized I really like Twitch," I admit, laughing bitterly. "But I know my brother won't allow it. And Twitch . . . he's such a good guy that he'll choose Mercedez's health over everything else. He'll do anything to keep her stable—even if it means making her his ol' lady to keep her quiet and to protect my relationship with my brother."

"She *what*?" Ivy squeaks, her voice rising in disbelief.

"Oh yes," I say, my voice dripping with sarcasm. "You can't make this stuff up. She threatened Twitch—told him to make her his ol' lady or she'd tell everyone about us. She even has proof of us kissing."

I fan my face, trying to calm the anger and hurt bubbling inside me. My heart feels like it's breaking all over again. "Why can't I ever be happy?" I ask, tears streaming down my face. "He's the only guy I've ever liked, and I can't have a relationship with him. I want more, and I hate myself for it because I know how this is going to end. I should be immune to the pain by now, but I'm not. The clubhouse was the only place I ever felt truly happy and at home. And now, with everything that's happened, it's all gone. Both Twitch and I are struggling with the lies and the deceit, but we're also struggling to say goodbye to each other. He was here last night, and then he had to leave because Mercedez called and threatened him."

"I'm so sorry, Milly," Ivy says sympathetically.

"Yes, I'm proud of my career and I'm content." I sniffle. "But being by myself isn't what makes me happy. My whole life is a litter of tiny papercuts on my heart, and just when I see happiness in my grasp, it slips away, leaving me with another cut."

"The whole Mercedez thing is crap." Ivy huffs. "Like, I get it, she's mentally unwell, but who does she think she is? And if she really cared about Twitch, she wouldn't be acting like this. She's just using him to get what she wants—to be an ol' lady. What are your thoughts on moving forward?"

My stomach twists painfully. "I don't think there's any moving forward for me and Twitch anymore. I understand the position he's in—he's trying to protect everyone, including me—but . . ." I slam my hand down onto the bed. "I want more. I want to be his first choice. I want him to put *us* above everyone else. I want him to fight for us."

"Why don't you tell him that?" Ivy asks gently.

"I'm worried about him," I admit. "He already looks like he's struggling, and I don't want to add to his stress. He hasn't had an easy life, and the MC pulled him out of a dark place. They're his family, and I know how important family is to him."

Ivy lets out a heavy breath. "Yeah, he's been keeping his distance and going to bed early. You can tell something's wrong when Twitch skips dinner. The men must know something's up, but they're probably thinking it's got to do with dealing with Mercedez."

My chest burns at the thought of Twitch being miserable. "I'm stuck," I whisper, my voice trembling. "The clubhouse was my safe place, and now, with Mercedez, it feels like I can't go back. I'm constantly walking on eggshells, afraid that one wrong look or conversation will push her over the edge and she'll tell Reaper. It's exhausting."

"You're always welcome here," Ivy says firmly. "But I get where you're coming from. Have you and Twitch thought about just saying 'screw it' and telling everyone? Dealing with whatever comes after?"

The thought of losing my brother sends a shiver down my spine. "It's a big deal. I have no one else left, and Twitch has only his mom and his brother."

"You'll always have me and Ava," Ivy says, her voice full of conviction.

"But you're part of the club," I counter. "If the club disowns me, they might not let you associate with me."

She huffs. "No one tells me who I can and can't talk to."

She has a point. The women in the club aren't pushovers. The men like to think they're in control, but the women are the real backbone.

"Don't write Twitch off just yet," Ivy says. "If he means that much to you, hold on a little longer."

TWITCH

I CAME STRAIGHT BACK TO THE CLUBHOUSE, WHERE MERCEDEZ was waiting for me. She was all smiles, acting like everything was perfect. I let her sleep in my bed, not wanting to cause a scene, but I warned her that I wasn't feeling well to avoid having to have sex with her. The look in Milly's eyes when I left her house last night keeps haunting me. All I wanted to do was stay. The thought of running away with her, far away from here, felt like a good idea, but Milly has her career and family here. She has a life. I can't take that away from her.

I was up the rest of the night, and the lack of sleep is taking a toll on me. It's not just the exhaustion—it's the stress. The constant pressure is suffocating, and I know it's only a matter of time before the lack of sleep starts affecting my epilepsy. I need to take better care of myself, but how can I when everything feels like it's falling apart?

Yes, I interrupted Milly's date last night, and for good reason. If I can't have her, no one can. I know she deserves someone like Edward—someone stable, someone who can give her the life she deserves. But the thought of her being with him makes my soul wither and die. I can't let it happen.

Now Mercedez is sitting on my lap while we watch TV,

and I feel utterly disgusted. It's like I need to scrub my skin raw just to get rid of the feeling. Everything about this feels wrong. Her touch repulses me. I'll never get over Milly, and I'll never forgive Mercedez for what she's done. All of this—her manipulation, her threats—it's all for what? To be an ol' lady?

Cash walks past, and I seize the opportunity to get Mercedez off me. "I need to get up and ask Cash to get you a cut," I say quietly.

She jumps up with a beaming smile, her excitement making my stomach churn. Just thinking about spending my life with her . . . it's dark, but maybe I'll need a knife for myself. I shake my head, trying to push the thought away. I've been spending too much time with Demon—his dark humor is rubbing off on me.

"Cash, do you have a minute?" I call out while he's going up the stairs.

He stops and turns, his expression curious. "Yeah, sure. What's up?"

I hesitate, my throat feeling tight and my tongue heavy. My body is rejecting the words before I even say them. But I have to do this. Cash patiently waits.

"Can you . . ." I pause, swallowing hard. "Can you get Mercedez a cut for being my ol' lady?"

Cash's eyes widen. "Since when has she been your ol' lady?"

"Since . . ." I trail off, my mind racing for an excuse. "Just recently."

He gives me a skeptical look. "I don't get involved in people's relationships, but as your friend . . . are you sure this is the right thing to do?" He scrunches up his nose, like he can't even believe what he's hearing.

In my head I'm screaming, *No, this is not the right thing to do!* But I force a smile, my muscles tense with the effort. "Yes, I'm sure."

Cash doesn't look convinced. "Sounds like you're trying to convince yourself more than me. For your own good, I'll let you sit on it for a bit. You haven't even told the club yet."

Milly needs her brother. He is her world. "No," I say with more confidence, "I'm sure."

He grimaces, clearly not buying it. "Okay, I'll order it for you. But you have to tell the club."

I nod. I don't have it in me to do it today. "I'll ask for a club meeting tomorrow."

He scratches his head, his expression still doubtful. "For what it's worth, I think you're making a shit decision."

I chuckle, though there's no humor in it. But what can I say? Yes, I know.

He shakes his head and walks away, leaving me alone with my thoughts. I head back to the lounge, my mind racing. How am I going to convince the club that I'm in love with Mercedez? Axle, Reaper, and Bomber will see right through it. They know me too well. But I don't have a choice. I have to come up with something.

Maybe I should tell Reaper I had sex with his sister. Surely death would be easier than the life I will have to endure with Mercedez.

FIFTEEN

ALL HELL BREAKS LOOSE

Twitch

FOR THE REMAINDER OF YESTERDAY, I WAS ON AUTOPILOT. I can't even remember what the conversations at dinner were about. It's all a blur. My mind has been consumed with one thing: convincing myself to tell the MC that I'm choosing Mercedez as my ol' lady. Last night I forced myself to organize a church meeting for ten this morning. The looks I got from everyone were odd—hell, I don't think I've ever called a meeting before. But I knew if I set it, I couldn't back out.

Even Ava asked if I was okay at dinner. I didn't miss the sad look Ivy gave me when she overheard. I'd love to ask her if she's spoken to Milly, but what those two talk about as friends is none of my business. Still, I'd give anything to be a fly on the wall during their conversations. Is Milly as torn up as I am? In a twisted way, I hope she is. I hope she's feeling my pain because that would mean she loves me.

I stand up from my computer chair, my heart pounding. *I*

fucking love her. Holy shit. The realization hits me hard. What the hell am I going to do now? I start pacing the room.

"Bro, it's ten," Axle says, leaning against the doorframe of the computer room. How has time gone so quickly this morning?

I'm sweating my ass off, trying to calm my frantic breathing. Pulling at my collar, I walk into church. I swear, the shirt feels too tight, like it's choking me. The other men walk in and take their seats. All eyes are on me. But I can't sit down—I'm too wired. I start pacing again.

Viper stands and puts a hand on my shoulder. "Man, are you all right?" His voice is full of concern, and I'm sure I look like a crazy person right now.

I pull at the neck of my shirt again, feeling like I can't breathe.

Axle whistles out loud. "Take it off, take it off!" he cheers in a mock-seductive voice.

Fuck this! I rip the shirt off over my head.

"Yewwww!" Axle cheers, wolf-whistling like an idiot.

There are a few chuckles, but most of the men are watching me with wide eyes.

"You called this meeting," Reaper points out to me. His tone is calm but firm, his eyes locked on me.

I clear my throat, but it doesn't help. My voice feels stuck, my chest tight. "I, umm . . ." My head swings back and forth, my thoughts racing between Milly and Mercedez. Death by Reaper or a life with Mercedez. Neither option feels survivable.

"I banged your sister," I blurt out.

The room goes dead silent. My brain struggles to process the fact that I just said that out loud. Around the table, everyone looks shocked—except for Demon, who's grinning like a lunatic.

"What did you just say?" Reaper's voice is low, almost

unworldly. He sounds confused, like he can't believe he has to ask again. But beneath the confusion, there's a clear threat of violence. His body is rigid, his eyes sharp as blades. If looks could kill, I'd be bleeding out on the floor right now.

Bomber's hand clamps down on Reaper's shoulder, holding him back. Shit, I'm in trouble. My eyes dart to the exit, considering my options.

"No, you didn't, you liar. Milly wouldn't sleep with you," Axle says with a smirk, clearly trying to lighten the mood.

The room is so quiet I can hear my own heartbeat pounding in my ears. It's deafening.

"That's why Milly hasn't wanted to come back to the club-house?" Reaper says, his voice low and dangerous, like he's piecing everything together. He stands, all six foot four of him, towering over the table. Bomber rises with him, his hand still firmly on Reaper's shoulder.

I gulp, watching the scene unfold in slow motion. Bomber tries to hold Reaper back, but it's no use. Reaper's arm pulls back, and a skull-shattering burst of pain explodes across my face. I hit the ground hard, the metallic taste of blood filling my mouth. Stars dance in my vision as shouting erupts around me.

"Are you still alive, you crazy son of a bitch?" Axle asks, crouching down beside me.

I blink a few times and his silhouette comes into focus, but I still can't see properly. I'm going to die, and I don't want to die a coward, so I croak out, "Help me up?"

Axle glances over his shoulder. "Nah, man, trust me. You want to stay down."

"No," I say, my voice firm despite the pain. "I need to tell Reaper the truth."

"You got a death wish?" Cash asks, standing beside me.

"I signed my death warrant when I slept with Milly," I reply, my voice steady.

Cash chuckles and extends a hand, helping me to my feet. My vision clears, but the throbbing in my face is relentless.

There's banging on the other side of the door at church. "What's going on in there?" Sophie asks.

"Reaper," Ava's voice follows. "Please come out. I'm worried."

Reaper's face is bright red. He's flanked by Bomber on one side and Viper on the other side. He doesn't answer her, and it's because he doesn't want to lie to her and say everything's alright when he wants to kill me.

"Everything's okay. It's club business," Bomber says sternly, his voice carrying authority.

The banging stops, and the room falls silent again. I take the opportunity to speak. "Look, it's not what you think. I fucking love Milly." My voice cracks with emotion. I wish I'd had the chance to tell her that before blurting it out to her brother.

"Don't you go lying," Reaper growls. The venom in his tone is expected, but fuck, it still hurts.

I point at him. "It's that what's been the problem!"

He cocks his head sideways. "What?"

"That look of betrayal and disappointment on your face, like we're the worst people on the planet. You wonder why we can't be together, why we kept it a secret and lied to everyone." I look around the table as I'm saying it. Then my gaze returns to Reaper. "It's because of you! We didn't want to upset you or betray you because we care, but I fucking love her, man."

"She's my sister!" he roars.

"She's the love of my life," I yell back, my voice echoing through the room.

Axle steps forward toward me, trying to defuse the situation. "We want to keep you alive. Don't poke the bear."

I've had a gutful. I'm always the nice guy. Even though I

shouldn't yell, my president has to hear me. Milly's the one for me.

Reaper shakes his head furiously. "I want more for her than anyone in the club can provide."

"What's so bad about us, Pres?" Viper asks. "You settled down with Ava."

"Milly got kidnapped because she was hanging around with people at the clubhouse!" Reaper's voice is tortured and raw, and now I get it. He still harbors guilt about Milly's kidnapping.

"It wasn't your fault she got kidnapped. It was Ivy's ex," Demon adds. I give him a small chin lift for the contribution, since he rarely talks or gets involved in things like this.

Reaper's shoulders sag slightly, the tension in his body easing. "It's not safe for her because of me," he mutters. "She already has a target on her. Being in a relationship with a club member would make it worse. I've always protected her."

"She's safer here with us than anywhere else," I argue. "When we thought she and Ivy were in danger, Demon and I found them and brought them home safely. I'll always protect Milly—with my life."

He crosses his arms and looks away.

"Milly told me you always protected her, but she's not a child anymore. I can make her happy. That should count for something, shouldn't it?" My voice softens at the end because deep down, he loves his sister, and he cares whether she's happy or not.

His eyes narrow as he processes my words. "How can you make her happy? If anything, I've never seen her so down and distant."

I run a hand down my face. "That wasn't my fault. Mercedez has been blackmailing me. That's the whole reason I called the meeting this morning. She threatened that if I didn't make her my ol' lady, she was going to tell everyone that she saw me and Milly kissing, so I folded. I didn't want to come between you and Milly, because she loves you and I didn't know how you'd react."

Reaper's face softens slightly, the fury in his eyes dimming as he listens.

"Look, don't take any of this out on Milly. It's all my fault. She's so scared of losing you and that you'll disown her, so blame me for everything," I say, my voice urgent. He has to understand that all this mess falls on me, not her.

I watch the anger dissipate from his face and the tension slowly drain from his body. He plonks down in his seat and lets out a deep breath, rubbing his temples. "Everyone leave. Give me and Twitch a moment."

Everyone hesitates for a beat before the men start filing out. Axle lingers, his eyes darting between me and Reaper. "Will Twitch still be breathing when he gets out?" he asks, half joking.

"Axle!" Reaper barks, and he hightails it out of the room.

"Take a seat," Reaper says, gesturing to the chair next to him.

I cautiously sit down, my body tense and ready for whatever comes next. Reaper cracks his neck from side to side.

"I love my sister," he begins, his voice low but steady. "It's been my job to protect her, and that's why I didn't want her involved with anyone in the club."

"But Milly's not a kid anymore," I say, my voice soft but firm. "I'd never do anything to hurt her. I've been trying to manage all this Mercedez drama too. I didn't want her to hurt herself, and I felt obligated to help her after everything we've been through. But I never asked Milly to leave the clubhouse. She did that on her own because she didn't want to trigger Mercedez. We're not horrible people, Reaper. We were just trying to do the right thing. But we couldn't help it—we fell for each other."

I lay it all out, my heart on the table. He needs to understand that we didn't lie to hurt him. We lied because we were scared of losing him.

Reaper rubs his chin, his expression thoughtful. "I get it now. I just wish you two had come to me first instead of letting it get to this point." He glances at my face and winces. "Sorry about the punch, but you slept with my sister, so you had it coming. At least you care about her and didn't just . . . you know."

The memory of my poor choice of words makes me cringe. "Yeah, saying 'I banged your sister' wasn't my finest moment. I panicked."

Reaper chuckles, and the tension in the room eases slightly. "I'd be panicked too."

I shrug, trying to lighten the mood. "What's one more punch to the face?"

His brows shoot up. "Who else hit you?"

"Mercedez, when she found out about me and Milly."

His face hardens, his tone turning serious. "You know I don't tolerate that kind of behavior. Mercedez has to go."

Relief washes over me, and for the first time in weeks, I feel like I can breathe. "What should I do? Call an ambulance and have it ready for when I tell her?"

Reaper shakes his head. "You're not going anywhere near her. I'll handle it. As president, I'll tell her she's no longer welcome here. She's not permitted to speak to anyone in the club or the ol' ladies. And yes, I'll organize for an ambulance to be here in case she tries to hurt herself again. But you need to cut ties completely. Block her number. Don't talk to her again. And Milly is to come back to the clubhouse so we can monitor her. I don't want Mercedez taking her revenge on Milly. I won't risk another situation like what happened with Sophie."

I nod, grateful for his support. "Thanks. Can the club

cover her doctor visits, medication, and anything else she needs to heal? I don't want her to feel abandoned, even after everything she's put me through."

Reaper nods. "That's fair. We'll make sure she gets the help she needs. But she can't stay here. Milly likes it here at the clubhouse, doesn't she?"

"She does love it," I say, a small smile tugging at my lips. "She says it feels like home."

Reaper's smiles. "That's good to hear. I like having her here."

"Everyone does," I add. With Mercedez and Reaper out of the equation, Milly and I can finally have a chance to be together—if she'll still have me. My head hangs low as doubt creeps in. "If I could go back, I'd tell Mercedez she couldn't manipulate me. And now that I know everything, I wish Milly and I had come to you first. To be honest"—I chuckle nervously—"we had no idea what my fate would be. No one's ever defied your orders before. I wasn't sure if I'd walk out of that conversation alive."

Reaper lets out a deep chuckle. "Don't get me wrong, I wanted to kill you when you said you banged Milly. Seriously, Twitch. You actually said the word *banged*."

"I panicked," I admit, feeling like an idiot.

Reaper shakes his head, a small smile on his lips. "Treat Milly well, Twitch, or I'll find a nice grave for you yet."

I swallow hard. "Duly noted." I stand, my resolve firm. "I'm going to talk to Milly."

"But she's at work," Reaper points out.

I shrug. "This can't wait. She needs to know everything now. You don't know what it's like to want to be with someone but feel like you can't."

Reaper's expression softens. "I know. Ava was married to an abusive husband."

"I feel such relief knowing we can finally be together," I say, pausing at the door. "With your blessing, of course."

Reaper nods. "As long as you protect her and make her happy. And it's a plus that she'll be living here, so my family can see her all the time. I'm sorry you felt like you couldn't come to me. I was so focused on keeping her safe that I didn't consider she'd be safest here with us—and with a man I trust."

A genuine smile spreads across my face. "Thank you, Pres. I understand your reasoning."

As I walk through the house, I feel the weight of the past few weeks lifting off my shoulders. I won't be here for the Mercedez finale. I have more important things to do. I hop on my bike, rev the throttle, and race toward the hospital, my heart pounding with anticipation. It's time to finally make Milly mine.

SIXTEEN
OUR LOVE IS
WORTH THE WAR

Milly

My phone vibrates with a message. I peek over to see it's
from Twitch.

Where are you?

Just at lunch. Why?

Where?

The hospital café. It's closest to the front
entrance of the hospital.

See you soon.

A buzz of electricity soars through me, wondering why
he's come to see me during my lunch break. As I finish the
remainder of my sandwich, commotion erupts. Screams echo
through the corridor, and I stand to see people running

toward the hospital entrance. My stomach drops as I spot Mr. Anders—the man whose wife died in the shooting—walking toward me, a gun cocked and aimed directly at me.

I gasp but force myself to stay composed even as my pulse thrashes against my skin. I scan the area. Nearly everyone has fled, leaving me alone with him. A security guard cautiously approaches, but I subtly raise my hand, signaling him to stay back. I don't want the situation to escalate.

As the old man walks closer, I see the hand holding the gun is trembling, which isn't good at all. It could go off at any moment. Tears stream down his face. "You killed my wife!" His voice is rough and broken.

I take a deep breath, calming my own panic. "What's your first name?" I ask softly.

"Terrence," he replies.

"Okay, Terrence," I say gently. "My name's Milly, and I want to say how deeply sorry I am for the grief you're experiencing. But your wife came to us with a gunshot wound that caused catastrophic injuries. Because of where the bullet hit her, no amount of medical skill could have saved her. We did everything we could." My voice is steady, but my heart is pounding. I need to humanize myself, to show him I care, but also to make him understand it wasn't my fault.

Out of the corner of my eye, I notice someone else in the corridor. It's Twitch. My body shakes with fear as our eyes lock. I give a small shake of my head, silently begging him to stay back. But his wide eyes and determined expression tell me he's not going to listen. He's moving closer, quietly and carefully. *No, Twitch. Please don't. I can't lose you.*

"No," Terrence says, his voice rising as he frowns. "You could have saved her, but you didn't."

"No, we couldn't have," I reply, keeping my tone calm. "It was the man who fired the gun through your house who's responsible, not anyone who tried to save her." I pause, hoping my words will sink in. "I can see she meant a lot to you."

"A lot?" he shouts, his voice breaking. "She was my world . . . now I have nothing to live for."

Twitch is closer now. His face is red. What happened? Terrence notices him and swings the gun toward him.

My heart hammers in my chest with such force it may explode. "No!" I yell.

Twitch has his arms up in surrender. "Hey, man, what's the problem?" Twitch asks in his easygoing voice. No stress lines it whatsoever. The tension in his shoulders gives him away. "Maybe I can help?" he offers.

Terrence shakes his head, his grip on the gun tightening. "My wife died. You can't help me. No one can, but this woman . . ." He points the gun back at me and I flinch. "She was supposed to save her, but she couldn't. Now I'm without my beautiful Dorothy," he says, his gaze dropping to his wedding ring.

"I'm sorry to hear about that," Twitch says, his voice steady. "But are you really here to kill a doctor who worked tirelessly to save Dorothy's life? Your wife wouldn't have wanted that."

Terrence's jaw tightens. "Someone must take responsibility. Someone has to suffer." His voice is tormented with a mix of pain and anger, but all I can think of is that person should be me, not Twitch. He has nothing to do with this.

"Kill me," Twitch says with a sad smile on his face as he glances at me. "Her name's Milly White, and she loves me."

I get teary-eyed as I shake my head, my eyes pleading. He can't do this to me!

Twitch steps closer to him. "So, if you want to hurt her, kill me and she'll suffer like you have."

Terrence's hand trembles as he shifts the gun between us, his face crumpling under the weight of his grief. More tears stream down his face as he suddenly points the gun at his own head.

A shiver rolls through me. Oh god, please, *no*.

"It should be me," Terrence says and briefly closes his eyes. "I can't live without my Dorothy."

"No!" I scream as Twitch lunges forward, grabbing the gun. Terrence falls to the floor in a heap, sobbing uncontrollably.

The security guard rushes forward and secures Terrence's arms behind his back. "Don't hurt him," I say. He's a grieving man; I don't wish any harm to him.

Twitch pulls me into a tight embrace, wrapping his arms around me protectively. He kisses the top of my head, his voice shaky. "I'm so happy you're okay."

"Me too," I reply, choked up as the tears flood my face. I whack his arm. "Don't ever do that to me again."

"I make no promises," he says, his tone turning serious. "Without you, life isn't worth living." He inches back, cupping my face in his hands. "I love you," he says, his voice thick with emotion, and kisses me again. "I fucking love you so much."

A rush of relief and joy flows through me from his declaration, and I sob into his chest, wetting his shirt. Once I settle down, I reply, "I love you too," though my voice is husky from crying. "You saved me . . . again."

He gazes at me with so much adoration it makes my heart ache. "I'll always be there for you," he says, brushing my tears away with his thumbs. "I told Reaper about us."

All the air leaves my lungs. "You what?" I ask, my voice barely above a whisper.

"Reaper knows," he says, his tone steady. "And he's okay with us being together. It's all going to be okay." He kisses my forehead. "I promise."

I stare at him, wide-eyed. "Are you kidding? Because this isn't funny."

He chuckles lightly. "I'm serious. I couldn't go through with the Mercedez lie. The thought of touching her repulses me. I've only ever wanted you. It hurts too much without you. I've wasted too much time trying to please everyone else. You're the most important person in my life. So I told Reaper I love his sister, and I'd do anything for her." He grabs my hand and places it over his chest. "Feel that? It beats only for you."

I feel the thump under my palm and swallow down the giant lump in my throat. Who knew he was this sweet? With his other hand, he rubs my back like he can't stop touching me. "I had to convince him that I could make you happy and that you'd be safe at the clubhouse."

I stare, stunned. Reaper knows . . . and he's okay with us being together. I cock my head to the side and touch his face where it's red. He flinches. "Let me guess—that punch is from my brother. Are you sure it's all okay?"

He grins, and it lights up his gorgeous face. "Yes, it was, but I deserved it. No more sneaking around. Just me and you . . . forever."

I'm still hesitant to accept it as truth. "We are talking about the same Reaper, right?" I ask, raising an eyebrow.

He ruffles my hair playfully. "Yes, we are."

A smile breaks across my face, and for the first time in what feels like forever, I feel the weight of the lies and secrets lift off my shoulders. "What about Mercedez?" I ask, my voice soft but cautious.

Twitch's expression hardens slightly. "Reaper is asking her to leave the clubhouse. He found out how she hit and manipulated me, and he wasn't happy. He's making sure she gets the help she needs, but she's not allowed to stay at the clubhouse or contact anyone in the club. He's even organizing an ambulance to be on standby in case she tries to hurt herself again."

I let out a long breath, the tension in my chest easing. "I'm glad she's getting help, but I'm even more relieved she won't be there anymore. I hated walking on eggshells around her."

Twitch sighs, running a hand through his hair. "I felt guilty for not confiding in Reaper sooner, but you know . . . self-preservation. I wasn't sure if I'd survive telling him about us. He looked like he wanted to kill me, and honestly, if I ever hurt you, he still might."

I giggle, the sound surprising even me. "Well, you'd better not hurt me, then."

He grabs my hand and kisses the top of it, his eyes softening. "I'll never hurt you again. I promise."

Before I can respond, Edward comes rushing out of the hospital, his face etched with concern. "Milly, I'm so sorry," he says, his voice full of sympathy. "I didn't realize he wanted to hurt you."

I place a reassuring hand on his shoulder. "It's okay, Edward. You didn't know. There's no need to apologize."

His shoulders sag with relief. "I'm glad you're okay."

The cops arrive shortly after, and Twitch and I give our statements. My manager pulls me aside and insists I take as much time off as I need. For once, I don't argue. I'm going to take this time to focus on myself and prioritize my happiness instead of burying myself in work.

WHEN WE ARRIVE BACK AT THE CLUBHOUSE, EVERYTHING SEEMS normal. No one is waiting for us outside, which tells me they don't know what happened at the hospital. If they did, Reaper, Ava, and Ivy would be out front to see if I was okay. I sit in the car a little longer, still apprehensive about facing Reaper now that he knows about me and Twitch.

Knock, knock.

Twitch is at my window. He opens the car door wide for me, and once I get out, he puts an arm over my shoulder, pulling me in close and kissing the side of my head. I feel lighter knowing he's by my side. He spoke up and stood up for us. Now it's my turn to reassure Reaper.

"Are you all right?" Twitch asks softly, concern lacing his voice.

I give him a small smile. "Yes," I reply, and we walk inside the clubhouse together.

The moment we step inside, the room falls silent. Everyone in the living area, by the pool table, and on the couches stops what they're doing to watch us. My heart pounds, nerves shooting through me. My poor heart is getting quite the workout today.

Axle whistles, breaking the silence. The ol' ladies clap and cheer. My cheeks heat, but I search for Reaper. He walks in from the kitchen and pauses, his eyes locking on me and Twitch. I gently pull away. "I'll be right back," I say to Twitch, who still looks concerned, and I walk to my brother.

When I reach him, I give him a tight hug, and he puts his arms around me, holding me firmly. "I'm so sorry for lying to you," I whisper, my voice trembling as I fight back tears.

He inches back, his hands resting on my shoulders. "No, I should be the one apologizing," he says, his voice heavy with regret. "I've always thought I was protecting you, but when you needed me most, you didn't feel like you could come to me. That's on me, not you. I thought I was doing the right thing, but I didn't realize I'd trust one of my brothers more than any stranger."

His words hit me hard, and I can hear the sadness in his voice. "Thank you for apologizing. I didn't want to disappoint you. Neither did Twitch. It was hard for him too. But there was no need to punch him," I add, giving him a pointed look.

He huffs, but before he can respond, Axle yells out, "Twitch told Reaper in the middle of the club meeting that he banged you." Axle laughs like a hyena, practically doubling over.

I gasp, appalled. "He did *not!*" I exclaim, turning to Twitch, who flinches and avoids my gaze. His guilty expression says it all.

Unbelievable. I scoff, crossing my arms. "No wonder you hit him," I mutter to Reaper.

"It was one of the funniest things I've ever heard," Viper chimes in, grinning.

My brother's face is stern. "It was *not* funny!"

I take a deep breath and address the room. "Something else happened today," I announce and wait until the room quietens. "A patient's husband—whose wife died of a gunshot wound a while ago—came to the hospital today with a gun and threatened to kill me." The room collectively gasps, and I quickly add, "Everything's okay. Twitch was there, and no one got hurt."

Reaper gives Twitch a chin lift, and I see it's out of respect. Ava and Ivy dash over to me and hug me tightly on either side. "I'm so grateful you're okay," Ava says, her voice full of relief.

"That's horrible," Ivy says, frowning. "You have had to go through another life-and-death situation."

"I'm okay," I assure them. "The old man was just grieving and in a lot of pain. I don't hold it against him."

Sophie, Elena, and Zara join us, and I give them a brief hug too.

"Still . . ." Sophie says, her tone curt. "Old man or not,

what he did was *not* okay. You're there to save lives and help people. What was he thinking?"

"I agree, but it's all over now, and I'm taking some much-needed time off work."

"Taking your own advice, are you?" Zara says with a sassy smile.

I jerk my head in a nod. "Yes, I am, and now they have a doctor to fill in for me."

"So no more McDaddy. What a shame," Sophie murmurs, pouting dramatically. She leans in closer, her voice dropping to a whisper. "But Twitch? Girl, he's hot—go get some!"

I laugh out loud, drawing some curious stares from the men. "I already had some," I say and give them a flirty wink.

Sophie whistles. "I need details."

"He's pierced," I whisper.

The group erupts into a mix of wide eyes, squeaks, and squeals.

I see Twitch making his way over to us, so I stand up straight and give him a sweet smile, pretending I wasn't just talking about his dick to everyone.

SEVENTEEN
MC FAMILY

Milly

One month has passed, and everything feels right with the world. Mercedez left the clubhouse the same day Twitch and I returned, and she hasn't been allowed back since. When Reaper broke the news to her, the women told me she threw a tantrum, yelling at him, but then broke down crying, begging to stay. Some of the women felt bad for her, but everyone knew it was the right decision.

The sweet butts said their goodbyes, and Bomber and Demon dropped her off at an old friend's house in a nearby suburb. I'm relieved it's over. Keeping secrets and constantly being on edge was exhausting. It drained me in ways I didn't even realize until it was over. Now I'm sleeping soundly in Twitch's bed, wrapped in his arms, without a care in the world.

I've been coping well with the near-shooting incident. No flashbacks, no nightmares—just peace. I think it's because Twitch has been by my side, making me feel safe and secure.

He's helped me overcome my fears. I didn't press charges against Terrence, but he had to go to court. I decided not to follow the case. I want to leave it all behind and focus on the future.

I haven't been back to work since, and honestly, it's been the best decision I've made in a long time. Reaper insisted I stay at the clubhouse, making it clear I wasn't to leave alone. First it was because of Mercedez, and now, after the shooting, he's being extra cautious. I've even caught him smiling at me and Twitch a few times, and I think he's finally accepted us. He sees how happy we are together.

Right now, Twitch and I are lying in his room, both in our pajamas, watching a trashy TV show. Through everything we've been through, our love hasn't been easy, but none of the good things in life ever are.

I'm lying on Twtich's chest when he asks, "When are you moving all your stuff to the clubhouse?"

A weird noise escapes my throat. "Why would I do that?"

"Because your home is here at the clubhouse," he says, sounding offended I even asked. "With me."

I blink, surprised. "The clubhouse feels like home. I just never thought of it." After getting most of the clothes from there, I haven't been back. "It seems like a waste of money, now that you've brought it up. Are you sure?" He's shown his commitment to me, but I have to double-check.

"I love you," he declares confidently. "And that's never going to change. I'll love you till the day you die, so yes, one hundred percent yes, I want you to move in."

"Aww . . . I love you too," I murmur, my heart swelling. He's so sweet. "Then, yes, I'll give up my rental and move the rest of my things in."

He kisses the top of my head. "That's what I like to hear. I know we've moved quickly, but I can't imagine my life without you. Oh, and I have a surprise for you too."

I get giddy with excitement. "When do I get my surprise?"

He grabs his phone. "In two hours it should arrive."

My mind races with possibilities as we finish the TV show. The anticipation is electric, and I count down the minutes until my surprise arrives.

Ava's dog Conan is barking outside, and I hear a truck pulling up. My heart races. "I wonder what it is."

Twitch stiffens. "You stay here." He glances back at me, his expression serious. "I mean it, Milly. Don't ruin the surprise. Just stay here."

"Okay," I mumble, disappointed but obedient. "I won't." He asked so nicely, how could I say no, even though I'm bouncing out of my skin with curiosity.

As he leaves, I glance around the room. My sweater is draped over the bedside table, my shoes are by the wall near the door, and my clothes are hanging in the closet. I've already moved myself in without even realizing it. Twitch has encouraged it every step of the way.

Without Mercedez, with everything right between me and Reaper, and with time off work, I've been so happy. I haven't slept this well in years. This is what living life should feel like —peaceful, exciting, and full of hope for the future. I'm finally focusing on myself, my happiness, and my journey. For so long, I was so busy fixing other people's lives that I forgot about my own.

Twitch walks back in with a beaming grin. "It's outside. Come on," he says, holding out a hand to help me stand.

I try to contain my excitement, but I feel like a kid on Christmas morning. We hold hands as we walk through the hallway and down the stairs. The clubhouse is oddly quiet, and I don't see anyone around. That is, until we step out the front.

Reaper and Cash are standing off to the side, and all the club men, their ol' ladies, and the sweet butts are gathered, smiling at me. My nerves spike as I glance at Twitch. "What's going on?"

He tugs on my hand, leading me through the crowd. People part to make way, and then I see it—a shiny, gorgeous black Harley-Davidson. My breath catches as I look at the bike, then back at Twitch, confused.

He leans down and kisses my forehead. "This bike is yours. Now you can practice on your own bike."

Something between a gasp and a high-pitched squeal comes from my mouth. My hands fly to my chest and my eyes water as I step closer to the bike. My hand goes to the handlebars, and I run my fingertips over the cold, smooth metal. Then I leap into Twitch's arms. "I love it, thank you so much!" The crowd cheers and claps, and my body hums with joy.

I don't remember a time anyone besides Reaper and Ava got me a present. Tears of happiness fall down my face.

Twitch frowns, brushing my tears away with his thumb. "I'm glad you like it, but don't cry," he says softly. "You deserve the bike, pretty lady. Wherever life takes us, I'm down for the ride. I'll go wherever you go."

Reaper walks over, his brows furrowed as he eyes the bike. "I didn't know you were learning to ride until Twitch told me," he says. Then he grumbles, "I wish you would have got her a less powerful bike."

I laugh, shaking my head. "Nope. This one is perfect." It looks like the men's bikes, just a bit smaller, probably lighter so I can control it more easily.

"You're missing something," Twitch says, walking over to Cash. He returns carrying a club vest. He holds it out to me. My smile grows wider, and my heart surges as I slip my arms through the armholes. The crowd cheers again.

My thumb brushes over the patch on the front that reads *Twitch's Property*, and more tears fall. Twitch hugs me tightly.

"Thank you," I whisper, my voice rough with emotion. I've always felt like I belonged here, but this vest makes it official. I'm Twitch's partner for life.

Twitch pulls back and goes to one knee. My body stills and my lungs are tight. "Holy shit," I mumble under my breath. This is all really happening.

"I've loved you from the moment I first saw you, and I'll love you till the day I die. You've always been the only one for me. Take my hand in marriage and I'll commit the rest of my life to protecting you and making you happy."

A sob breaks free as I nod frantically. "Yes, of course!" He slides a beautiful gold ring with a pear-shaped diamond onto my finger.

He stands, and I whisper, "Pinch me."

He cocks his head to the side and laughs. "No."

"This all feels like a dream. It doesn't feel real."

He gives me a firm kiss on the lips. "It's real, baby."

Axle's voice cuts through the moment. "You're an over-achiever, Twitch, trying to make us all look bad."

The crowd chuckles, and I glance around at the familiar faces. Everyone's different, and that's what makes this place feel like home. Reaper and Ava have a child together, Bomber and Zara are married with a baby on the way, Viper and Sophie accidentally got married but seem happier than ever, and Elena and Axle are perfectly content as they are. Even Demon and Ivy, with their quiet, intense connection, seem to have found their own version of happiness. Not everyone needs a ring to prove their love, but for me and Twitch, this feels right.

Reaper makes his way over to us, his expression softer than I expected. He pulls me into a hug, holding me tightly.

"You approved this?" I ask, glancing at my ring with a teasing smile. I know Twitch would've made the effort to talk to him first.

Reaper shrugs, a small smile tugging at his lips. "You two seem happier than ever, and Twitch has proven time and time again that he'll protect you. I can't ask for much more than that. Plus," he adds with a smirk, "Ava's been in my ear about not interfering and letting you make your own decisions. And honestly, it'll be nice to have your face around the clubhouse on a permanent basis."

I hug him tighter. "Thank you," I say sincerely.

As I pull back, I notice the ol' ladies gathered to my left, their eyes sparkling with joy. I turn to them while the men move to shake hands with Twitch.

"Show me, show me!" Sophie says eagerly, practically bouncing on her toes.

I hold out my hand, and the women crowd around in a chorus of "oohs" and "ahhs."

"The ring is beautiful," Ivy gushes, her eyes wide. "I'm so happy I got to be a part of your special day."

Ava steps forward, pulling me into a warm hug. When she pulls back, I notice tears streaming down her face. "Aww, don't cry," I say, my own eyes threatening to water again.

She quickly brushes the tears away, laughing softly. "Like Ivy said, I'm just so happy to be a part of today. Seeing you and Reaper happy—it's a beautiful sight."

Her words strike me right in the heart. She's such a kind, empathetic person, and my brother is so lucky to have her. "Thank you," I whisper, squeezing her hand.

"Yay!" Elena beams, clapping her hands together. "You finally got your vest. It suits you so well."

I grin, pulling the vest tighter around me. "It feels amazing." I do a playful runway turn, earning chuckles from the group.

"Now you're officially part of the family," Zara says with a warm smile.

"Yes, I do feel like I belong," I reply, my voice thick with emotion. My heart feels full, like it might burst from all the love and support surrounding me. I glance over at my bike, my smile widening. "And how sexy is my new ride?" I add with a laugh.

The women cheer, their excitement infectious.

"I didn't know you were learning to ride," Zara says, her tone curious.

"I've always wanted to," I admit. "Twitch taught me first, and I couldn't get enough. I needed a hobby, something to focus on outside of work. Riding has been perfect."

"I'm so jealous," Sophie murmurs, her eyes locked on my bike. Then she yells across the yard, "Viper!" He glances over, raising an eyebrow. "I want one!" she declares, pointing at my Harley.

Viper laughs, shaking his head. "We'll see," he says, but the amused look on his face tells me Sophie will probably get her way.

"I'll take that as a yes," Sophie says confidently, crossing her arms.

"It'll be fun to have another woman to ride with." I laugh, imagining the two of us cruising down the road together. "I'd love that."

As the celebration continues that evening, I find myself surrounded by the people I care about most. The ol' ladies are already planning a celebratory dinner, and the sweet butts are chatting excitedly about the engagement.

Twitch makes his way back to me, his eyes soft and full of love. He wraps an arm around my waist, pulling me close. "Are you okay?" he asks, his voice low and intimate.

I nod, leaning into him. "I'm more than okay. I'm happy."

He smiles and brushes his thumb over my cheek. "Good. That's all I want."

Reaper approaches us again, his expression serious but

not unkind. "Twitch," he says, his tone firm. "Take care of her."

Twitch straightens, his grip on me tightening slightly. "Always."

Reaper nods, satisfied, and turns to me. "And you—don't let him get away with anything."

I laugh, the sound light and carefree. "Don't worry, I won't."

Reaper smirks, then pulls me into another hug. "I'm proud of you, Milly. You've been through a lot, but you've come out stronger. You deserve this happiness."

Tears prick my eyes again, but I blink them away. "Thank you," I whisper, my voice thick with emotion.

EIGHTEEN
PARTY TIME

Milly

A week after Twitch proposed, we decided to throw an engagement party. Twitch is eager to get married as soon as possible, and honestly, I'm just as excited. We chose a local bar for the celebration so everyone could relax, enjoy themselves, and not have to worry about cooking or cleaning. The ol' ladies took charge of decorating the entertainment room, filling it with balloons, streamers, and a big Congratulations sign. They even hired a DJ, which has added a fun, lively vibe to the night.

A waiter walks over with a tray of champagne glasses, and I take one, savoring the feeling of being wined and dined. "Thank you," I say with a smile, and take a small sip. The bubbles tickle my nose, and I glance around the room, soaking in the joy and laughter of everyone here to celebrate with us.

I've been planning another vacation with Twitch, but this time, I'm paying for it. I earn good money, and I want him to know that I value him and our relationship. He doesn't need to feel like the sole provider—I'm a successful woman, and I want to contribute just as much as he does. It's important to me that he knows we're equals in this partnership.

"You look beautiful," Ava says, pulling me from my thoughts. She's standing beside me, her smile making me feel even more confident.

"Thank you," I reply, glancing down at my dress. I bought it specifically for tonight—a navy blue cocktail dress with a V neckline and flutter sleeves. "I've never spent this much on a dress before, but Sophie talked me into it. She was adamant it was made for me."

Ava chuckles. "She was right. You look stunning."

"Do you like the heels?" I ask, extending my leg to show them off. I rarely wear heels, but these matched the dress perfectly, and I have to admit, I like how they make me feel.

"I love them," Ava says, her eyes sparkling. "You've really gotten your confidence back. You're glowing."

Her words warm my heart. "I really appreciate that," I say, glancing down at my engagement ring. "I've never felt this good."

"It's because you found the right person to spend your life with," Ava says softly. "I settled for my first husband, and it was the worst mistake of my life. He made me feel like a failure, no matter how hard I tried. But with Reaper . . ." She lets out a contented sigh, her smile growing. "He makes me feel beautiful and wanted. He's shown me what love truly is. When you feel true love, you just know you're meant to be with that person forever."

Her words resonate deeply with me. Twitch has always made me feel beautiful, even when I'm in sweatpants with a messy bun. He's never made me feel like I had to be anything other than myself.

Zara walks over, her hands resting on her round belly.

She looks radiant, and I can't help but smile. "How far along are you now?" I ask, reaching out to gently touch her belly.

"Five months," she replies, her face glowing with happiness.

Ava and I both rub her belly, and I chuckle. "I love pregnant bellies," I say. It's such a sweet, special time, and seeing Zara like this makes me think about how fast everything has happened with Twitch. It's been a whirlwind, but I wouldn't change a thing.

As I glance around the room, I take in the smiling faces of our friends and family. Everyone is chatting, laughing, and enjoying themselves. The DJ is playing soft music, and the atmosphere is great. Sophie walks back from the DJ booth with a mischievous grin on her face.

"Do you have a song request?" she asks, leaning in conspiratorially. "Quick, before the men take over the playlist."

"'Bonnie and Clyde' by Phix," I say without hesitation. It's a fun, upbeat song that reminds me of my relationship with Twitch—wild, passionate, and unbreakable.

Sophie grins and heads back to the DJ. Moments later, the song starts playing, and she grabs the microphone. "Everyone!" she calls out, her voice cutting through the chatter. The room quiets, and all eyes turn to her. "This song is for Twitch and Milly." She raises her glass high. "Congratulations, you two lovebirds!"

The room erupts in cheers and applause, and Twitch makes his way over to me. He's dressed in his usual club attire, and I love him for it. He doesn't need to dress up or prove anything—he's perfect just the way he is. He pulls me close, his lips brushing mine in a brief but tender kiss.

"I can't wait to get you out of this dress," he murmurs, his voice low and full of promise.

I throw my head back, laughing. "I could tell by the way you've been ogling me all night."

He scoffs, his lips curving into a pout. "Have you seen how drop-dead gorgeous you look? You should be wearing your property patch."

"Over this?" I ask, glancing down at my dress.

He nods, his expression serious. "Yes, so every man in this place knows you're mine."

I roll my eyes at his overprotectiveness, but secretly, I love it. "I need to go to the restroom," I say, setting my glass down on a nearby table. "I'll be right back."

"Do I need to fight every man who tries to talk to you outside this room?" he teases, his tone playful but with a hint of seriousness.

I laugh, swatting his arm. "Twitch, stop it. I'll be right back."

As I step outside of the entertainment area, I walk past the bar and pause. A beautiful woman wearing a long wedding dress is sitting there. I peer around. It doesn't look like a bridal party is here, which is strange. As I walk closer, I can see she's been crying. My stomach drops, thinking something horrible has happened to her.

To my surprise, as I'm walking past, I see Rage sitting next to her. She gives him a small smile, and it warms my heart that he's trying to comfort this poor woman and make her smile. He's such a great guy, but it has me wondering if anything will come of it.

I don't linger, not wanting to intrude on their moment. Instead, I head to the restroom. Tonight has been perfect so far, and I can't help but feel grateful for everything—the love, the laughter, and the people who make my life so full.

The end.

. . .

A sneak peek of Rage and Rose's story is next.

Did you want to go into the draw to win a free paperback? Sign up for my mailing list. Simply opening my newsletter emails enters you to win any paperback.

If you love my books, please leave a review or rating on your purchased retailer or your favorite platform. It encourages other readers to take a chance on me. It truly makes a difference and provides crucial feedback.

SNEAK PEEK AT RAGE

Rose

The bartender places the drink in front of me. "Here, ma'am. The first one's on the house."

I smile at him, grateful for his kindness. "Thank you." I bring the cold drink to my lips and gulp it all down until only ice remains in the glass. It's sweet and refreshing, but nowhere near enough. I slide the glass back to him. "I'll take another."

He doesn't hesitate. I smash that one too and request another because there's still a strong ache in my chest.

What I don't understand is Tyler. How can he say he loves me one night but cheat on me with my best friend the next? That's not love. My stomach is in knots as I replay the last few years. I can't believe I was so blindsided. I thought I was lucky that my best friend and partner got along so well. My cheeks heat with embarrassment.

My family, friends, and everyone in my hometown are going to find out the truth. I'm going to be the clueless woman who didn't see it. Did anyone else know? I rub my chest. They waited for the worst possible time to tell me, embarrassing me like that. Why didn't Tyler just leave me and go be with her? Why let it get to my wedding day? I wasted so many years with him. The air-conditioning is cool inside the bar area, but I just feel cold . . . all the way to my broken heart.

A chair scrapes beside me and a deep voice cuts through my thoughts. "I'll take a beer," the man says to the bartender. "And another drink for the bride."

Please don't talk to me. Please don't talk to me.

"Is anyone sitting here?" he asks.

I glance around. Yep, he's talking to me. *God damn it!* I look up at him—and freeze, staring deep into a younger man's ocean-blue eyes. Both stormy and intense. He's gorgeous.

"No, it's free," I say, giving him a tight smile.

"Did you just get married?" he asks, his tone curious.

Screw it. I'm feeling a little lighter from the alcohol. "Nope . . . instead I found out my best friend has been screwing my partner for a year, and she decided to tell me right before I was due to walk down the aisle."

His face falls. "I'm so sorry," he says, and it sounds genuine. "I hate cheaters."

Goosebumps erupt over my arms. We agree on something.

His brows pull in. "Are you cold?"

Before I can answer, he slips out of his hoodie and passes it to me. I can smell his cologne. It's refreshing but has a bold masculine scent. "Thank you," I say softly, and slip it over my curled hair. His hoodie is warm, and even though I'm a big girl, it still fits me.

I glance down at my attire. A puff of air escapes me. "I'm a wreck with a hoodie on over the top of a fancy wedding dress. Real classy."

"Nah," he says, his lips curving into a smile. "You look sexy."

The compliment catches me off guard, and I dissolve on the spot. But is he saying it out of sympathy? "Thank you for being nice to me. You go and enjoy your night. I'll be at the bar whenever you want your hoodie back." Let's face it—I'll be here till they close.

He shakes his head, a small, confident smile tugging at his lips. "I'm not going anywhere."

I take a proper look at him. He's tall—easily over six feet —with thick, slightly tousled hair and a five-o'clock shadow that gives him a rugged look. His eyes hold mine for a beat too long. My pulse quickens. I glance around the bar, taking in the groups of women scattered at tables, all of them gorgeous. What's he doing here, talking to the bigger girl in a wedding dress?

"It's okay," I say, my voice soft. "You don't have to stay because you feel bad for me." He seems like a nice guy, but he's clearly younger than me. How much younger? It's hard to tell.

His lips lift slightly, a hint of amusement in his expression. "No, I want to stay."

My heart flutters, betraying me. The most handsome young man I've ever seen wants to talk to me. I don't have it in me to tell him to leave. It's better to have someone here so I don't feel lonely.

I glance down at his outfit—a crisp white shirt under a leather vest, paired with baggy jeans. Simple, but it suits him. Too well. I chastise myself for noticing. I just found out my fiancé cheated on me, and here I am, flustered over a stranger. I would never cheat—not that Tyler and I are together now— but I can't seem to control the way my body reacts to him. Maybe the alcohol is just numbing the pain of their betrayal.

"What's your name?" I ask, my voice steadier than I feel.

"Theo," he says, extending a hand. "And yours?"

"Rose." I slip my hand into his, and the moment our skin touches, a jolt of electricity zips through me. I pull back slightly, startled by the intensity of it. Guilt creeps in, but there's a small voice in the back of my mind whispering, *Why not?* Tyler cheated on me, and here's this kind, attractive man who actually wants to talk to me. Why should I feel bad about that?

"Are you just here for a few drinks?" I ask, desperate to keep the conversation going.

"I'm at an engagement party for my friends, Milly and Twitch," he says, gesturing vaguely toward the other side of the bar. "But I don't really feel like celebrating right now. I just wanted a couple of drinks to unwind."

The bartender places our drinks in front of us, and I take a sip through the straw, trying to appear more composed than I feel. The sweet, tangy flavor cools me down, though I'm still hyperaware of Theo's presence beside me.

"What have you got there?" he asks, nodding toward my purple drink.

"A fruit tingle," I reply.

He tilts his head, intrigued. "It looks good."

"Want a taste?" The words tumble out before I can stop them, and my cheeks heat instantly. I can't believe I just said that.

Theo's smile widens, warm and disarming. He leans closer, his lips brushing the straw as he takes a sip. My body stiffens, every nerve on high alert.

He leans back, smirking. "Yeah, it's good. A bit strong, though."

I shrug, trying to play it cool. "I need strong drinks tonight."

He raises his hands in mock surrender, chuckling. "Completely understandable."

I can't help but smile at his playfulness. "So, tell me about yourself, Theo. Anything to get my mind off the nightmare I'm living."

"At least you found out now," he says, his tone serious. "Did you have kids with him?"

"No." I'm grateful for that small mercy. But the thought lingers—if Kayla hadn't told me, how far would Tyler have let it go?

"That's good," Theo says, his voice tinged with something darker. "Nothing worse than dragging kids through it."

There's a weight to his words, a bitterness that makes me wonder if he's speaking from experience. I take another sip of my drink, letting the alcohol steady me. "I just can't believe it," I admit. "I wasted four years being the perfect partner, doing everything I could to make him happy. I worked full-time, but I also cleaned the house and made his dinners, his lunches—everything. He didn't have to lift a finger, and it still wasn't enough." My voice wavers, and I straighten my back, determined not to cry again.

He places a hand on my arm, and I look into soft eyes. "It has nothing to do with you and everything to do with him. He sounds like a loser, and you sound like his mom. And that so-called friend of yours was never a friend anyway and eventually showed you her true colors. People always do."

His words hit me like a revelation. He's right. For the first time, I realize I did and gave too much, and it was never reciprocated. The fault wasn't mine.

"Do you have a girlfriend?" I ask, the alcohol taking over.

"I surely don't," he says in an upbeat tone.

A hint maybe? *Pfft . . . who am I kidding? A young man like him wanting me? Impossible.*

"Well . . . a bit about me. I'm in a motorcycle club." He looks down at his vest.

My tongue feels heavy. "Is it . . . a bad club?" I lean toward him, tipsy and curious. "Do you kill people?"

He laughs. The sound is rich and warm, and it lightens something in me.

"We're the good type. We look out for people in the community."

I don't know what he means by that, but I like the sound of it. "How old are you?" He's clearly a man, but younger than me. I'm just not sure how much.

He smiles, and it's glorious. "Old enough."

"Old enough for what?" I tease.

"For you."

My body ignites and I forget how to breathe for a second. He's ballsy, but not arrogant. My nipples pebble against my bra. His eyes smolder, and I get lost in them. Thoughts flicker. *What have I got to lose? Nothing.*

"Let's get a room," he says, holding out his hand.

A bolt of lust overcomes me, leaving me giddy. I place my hand in his. His eyes roam over me with a fierce hunger I've never seen any man have before, and it sends a ripple down my spine. He looks at me like he wants me, but I'm just *me* . . . I'm all curves. Pudgy belly, thick thighs. Why would someone like him want me? But he couldn't fake the longing in his eyes that says he wants me.

He leans in, his breath warm against my neck. "Don't tell me you're gonna back out . . . I'm already hard for you."

And just like that, all the toxic thoughts leave me. Butterflies take over my stomach.

"Okay," I whisper as adrenaline soars through me. A sexy distraction to take my mind off the pain stalking me tonight.

Grab your copy of Rage now.

RESOURCES

One Australian dollar of every paperback book purchase from Bianca's website will go to the LifeLine charity.

If you are struggling with your mental health, contact Life-Line. LifeLine is available in many countries and offers help for people experiencing emotional distress. They provide confidential crisis support, and in most instances, you can call, chat online, or text.

Please visit https://lifeline-intl.com/our-network/ for more information.

If you are seeking help with a drinking problem, contact Alcoholics Anonymous. AA is an informal society that operates in many countries and offers peer support for recovery from alcoholism.

Please visit https://www.aa.org/find-aa/world for more information.